PENGUIN BOOKS

NOCTURNES FOR THE KING OF NAPLES

Edmund White teaches writing at Johns Hopkins University and has been an editor of *Saturday Review* and *Horizon*. His writing has appeared in publications such as *Poetry*, *Art in America*, *Harper's*, *The New Republic*, and the *Washington Post*. With Charles Silverstein he is co-author of *The Joy of Gay Sex*. A rare combination of poetic language and ironic humor, his first novel, *Forgetting Elena*, has received considerable critical acclaim.

NOCTURNES
for the
KING of NAPLES

EDMUND WHITE

PENGUIN BOOKS

Penguin Books Ltd, Harmondsworth,
Middlesex, England
Penguin Books, 625 Madison Avenue,
New York, New York 10022, U.S.A.
Penguin Books Australia Ltd, Ringwood,
Victoria, Australia
Penguin Books Canada Limited, 2801 John Street,
Markham, Ontario, Canada L3R 1B4
Penguin Books (N.Z.) Ltd, 182–190 Wairau Road,
Auckland 10, New Zealand

First published in the United States of America by
St. Martin's Press 1978
Published in Penguin Books 1980

Copyright © Edmund White, 1978
All rights reserved

LIBRARY OF CONGRESS CATALOGING IN PUBLICATION DATA
White, Edmund, 1940–
Nocturnes for the King of Naples.
I.   Title.
[PZ4.W5829NO   1980]   [PS3573.H463]   813′.5′4   79-22059
ISBN 0 14 00.5330 1

Printed in the United States of America by
Offset Paperback Mfrs., Inc., Dallas, Pennsylvania
Set in Baskerville

Except in the United States of America,
this book is sold subject to the condition
that it shall not, by way of trade or otherwise,
be lent, re-sold, hired out, or otherwise circulated
without the publisher's prior consent in any form of
binding or cover other than that in which it is
published and without a similar condition
including this condition being imposed
on the subsequent purchaser

To David Kalstone

Parts of this book have appeared in *The Chicago Review, Christopher Street* magazine, and *Shenandoah*.

The author gratefully acknowledges the support of the Ingram Merrill Foundation.

> The abstract joy,
> The half-read wisdom of daemonic images,
> Suffice the ageing man as once the growing boy.

W. B. Yeats, "Meditations in Time of Civil War."

NOCTURNES for the KING of NAPLES

CHAPTER I

A young man leans with one shoulder against the wall, and his slender body remains motionless against the huge open slab of night sky and night water behind him. He is facing the river. Little waves scuttling shoreward from a passing, passed scow slap against boards: perfunctory applause. On the other side of the water, lights trace senseless paths up across hills, lash-marks left by an amateur whip. He turns toward me a look of hope tempered by discretion, eyes dilated by a longing too large—as large as this briny night panel behind him—to focus in on any single human being.

I have failed to interest him. He turns back to his river as though it were the masterpiece and I the retreating guard.

For me there was the deeper vastness of the enclosed, ruined cathedral I was entering. Soaring above me hung the pitched roof, wings on the downstroke, its windows broken and lying at my feet.

A wind said incantations and hypnotized a match flame up out of someone's cupped hands. Now the flame went out and only the cigarette pulsed, each draw molding gold leaf to cheekbones.

There are qualities of darkness, the darkness of

gray silk stretched taut to form the sky, watered by city lights, the darkness of black quartz boiling to make a river, and the penciled figures of men in the distance, minute figures on—is that a second story? What are they doing up there? A cigarette rhymes its glow with my own across the huge expanse that has shattered its crystal lining to the ground.

I told myself to stand still in the shadow of an immobile crane, its teeth rusted shut, to stand still and watch. What I was looking for were the other men secreted in corners, or posted on dilapidated stairs, or only half-visible behind tarred bollards. The wind died and in my hiding place a bowl of fragrances was lifted like a potpourri culled from leaves, cloves, tar, burned rubber—droll hobby. I could scarcely get past the preserving odor of brine. But just beneath it hovered the smell of trapped sweat on bodies. Beneath everything else I smelled (or rather heard) the melancholy of an old, waterlogged industrial building, a sound as virile but at the same time as sexless as a Russian basso descending liturgically from low G to F to E, on and on down on narrow steps below the stave into a resonant deep C.

The men I was searching for now became palpable. They leaned out of the low shelf of night. They whispered, if they were in twos, or shifted their weight from foot to tentative foot if alone. At the far end of the vaulted room in a second-story window, one gnat-sized man knelt before another.

I had moved out from under the crane to walk the length of the pier, intrigued by the symmetrical placement of people on the far-away landing deck. They stood at attention, motionless—ah! posts. They were posts, but the sound beside my right hand was human breathing. Through the glassless window of an office I saw a man sitting on the floor, breathing. I didn't speak but rather rested my hand on the sill, which was grained as fur. He plopped his hand over mine: not dry, not clean. Beneath the concealing ridge of his brow his eyes could have been staring up at me.

Congeries of bodies; the slow, blind tread on sloped steps; the faces floating up like thoughts out of ink, then trailing away like thoughts out of memory; entrances and exits; the dignified advance and retreat as an approaching car on the highway outside casts headlights through the window and plants a faint square on the wall. The square brightens till it blazes, then rotates into a trapezoid narrowing to the point of extinction, its last spark igniting a hand raised to hit a face. A new square grows on the wall but when it veers off it reveals not the stunned face, nor the punishing hand—ooze on old boards, nothing else.

Down the steps, past the polite, embarrassed face of someone I know. I mount a loading ramp onto a platform where an insubstantial shack, doorless and windowless, shelters another cigarette. I stop at the doorway. He turns to the wall, causing me to retreat. There is another dubious figure, tall, face visored. I won't risk encountering him now. He can wait—that he·*will* wait is the bet I'm willing to place. A shed at the extreme end of the platform glistens and sweats with water; running water can be heard, muted, sloshing through moss-slick pilings. Into that wet vault I take a step. A hand; a bearded face; the smell of whiskey; another hand. My motionless shoes turn cold—no, wet. A vagrant wave wallops against the pier like a blanket someone shakes out during spring cleaning. A boy with pale arms bruised by shadow is caught in the cross-currents of fear and curiosity. Something behind me is ticking, an electrical timer in good running order within a building I had assumed was long ago defunct.

Retracing my steps, I notice that the sentinel I'd left posted by the door to the shack has been relieved but not replaced. Down a ramp I go into the central hall, which not only reports but also magnifies the waves drumming the dock in triplets of eighths over the sustained crescendo-diminuendo of a passing barge. As it passes, the barge pivots its spotlight into our immense darkness; two voices, male, call back and forth to one another from bow to stern over tons of clean gravel. Instructions. Orders.

Our orders, scattered by the prying beam, emerge out of hiding places. A hand-rail, wrenched away from the stairs it was designed to guard, stencils opposed pairs of black S's on absorbent gray air. A protective sheathing of corrugated tin, torn free from the clerestory, rattles stage thunder above us.

Yes—us. A moment before the barge's beam invaded the cathedral we were isolated men at prayer, that man by the font (rainwater stagnant in the lid of a barrel), and this one in a side chapel (the damp vault), that pair of celebrants holding up a flame near the dome, those communicants telling beads or buttons pierced through denim, the greater number shuffling through, ignoring everything in their search for the god among us.

This glorious image I've made, sustained like a baldachino on points of shadow above the glass mosaic on the floor, gently folds under the sun. The sun is rising. It recalls us to work, play, reputation, plans, to guilt, and sends everyone away until only I remain, hugging my knees, my eyes unfocused into the refracted dazzle of water. The red line painted on a boat's hull rises and dips, its reflections flaring on the waves like flames from the sun's corona, scorching the mystic vacuum.

On my way home I see one last man pressed against the wall, gathering about him the last tatters of darkness to be had. He is very rough with me.

"Do you want to go to my place?" he asks.

"Yes."

"Promise you won't change your mind when you see me in the light?"

"Do I know you?"

"Promise?"

I nod.

And then, once we're in the light, I see he's one of your old admirers, the crazy one who gave you the dog. We smile and begin to talk about you.

In that lady's house we were all standing in the July heat. Encased in my white suit, tie, shirt, I stood very still and felt the sweat explore my body.

5

That afternoon I was handsome and drunk. The glare on the water outside projected a rippling shoal on the ceiling of her salon. Motorboats just outside the open windows plunged noisily by.

I stood there intrigued by the sweat secretly bathing my chest, as though the thinnest, purest stream of silver, poured over its living model, were hardening into flexible armor against—against doing anything. I nodded to the woman who had found me and asked her another question about— well, her jewelry, why not her jewelry, that antique jewelry? Behind me stood my father. He did not recognize me and I kept hesitating to introduce myself.

He did not seem to know the language of this place, and the girl with him had to translate everything. She did it charmingly, interpolating compliments.

Our shoulders touched. While listening to the woman with the old necklace, I had shifted my stance ever so slightly until I brushed against my father. Naturally he drew away—he was here to talk to everyone simply and openly, but not to touch them.

Where had he just come from? And who was the girl? Returning from the bar I slumped into a white cane-bottomed chair and ran the fingers of my left hand over the bulges calculated to simulate joints of bamboo. Like the clearest French olive oil, the sunlight fried on the dark water. The plant beside me had been stretched taut on strings as though it were a vine, or would be, and I fingered

6

one of its cool, heart-shaped leaves and hairless stems.

No one was bothered by my retreat into the chair. People were content, I suppose, to have seen another young man, his face handsome enough to explain why he might have been invited.

My father didn't recognize me. That made me become all the more a white suit and tanned hands and face. Once, when I was a child, I had seen him consult a list of six points to cover during lunch and only after coffee did I realize, with a chill, that he had indeed touched, or led others to touch, all six points. Not even his stammer could be trusted since it was only a ruse he had devised to force other men to finish his ambiguous sentences for him. His decision to ignore an adult son might easily have been just such a strategem, a sacrifice to vanity, to his own ageless face.

There are qualities of light: the light heightened by the sheer curtains, made as pure as the napkin over the host by these folds in the tablecloth, or the light freshly revived in the ruche of that blouse or caught in the gray, splintered fern in my ice cube. The bands of silk and velvet striping that S-shaped couch they call a *causerie* lit and extinguished the light in rapid succession, the velvet grained like fur, the silk as wind.

The girl with my father, yes, reminded me of myself. She was one more functionary he had drummed up, a pretty face, as pretty as Linda's or mine might have been when I was sixteen and he leaned over the table and said softly, "A boy your

7

age could be a girl." Later he said, "You have your mother's eyes."

As I looked around the room I prized the blown glass figures behind the vitrine, our hostess's folly, things she would never have commissioned while her husband was still her husband, but which now, between solitude and senility, she had succumbed to because the blue objects were . . . "pretty." As indeed they and we and, now, I were, the unrecognizable face above the white shirt front that disguised the rivulets of sweat collecting at the clavicle and then coursing down my body. He was capable of ignoring me if it suited his purposes.

He'd always had purposes: his own amusement, or failing that, relief from boredom. And like a child staring through the back window of a family car at the last lights of the party where for the first time he has seen two men hold hands a second too long—like that child I returned to the open door.

Standing, I hold myself in tight reserve. If his talent let him cover all points, then mine instructed me to wait, not see the meanings exposed in broad gesturing, nor did I take the slightest pains to make *me* evident in gestures big or small. I find and light an old, bent, damp Pall Mall—till now I was keeping it in reserve. A bare-legged boy lifts a guitar to make a sound that draws attention from all points and silences the crowd. Then, gesturing, he halloos a friend back from the sea. He strikes a flat A first, now sharp C, now F. I let myself forget it all, good times, good sex, good food; gesturing farewell, I spend my past without reserve, a pauper king, whom every subject points to—but that's a fantasy I

8

make in idle moments, and I'm sure to make them each as idle as the evening sea's become beyond the masts, beyond the points of architectural lace, under the small but rising wind. "They're about to serve," our hostess tells everyone, gesturing.

"Look at the poor old thing there, gesturing at all these perfect strangers. What can make her do it night after night? What reserves of habit is she drawing on that see her through another dull party at all?"

"Entertaining's not one of her strong points."

Useless as a sundial in shade that points gray on gray, I keep from gesturing (or am kept) by luxurious if small delights in poverty from wanting to make the signs that others would be sure to see as telling. Hold yourself in deep reserve. At so many points I wanted to serve myself up and then, gesturing, to call out. But I don't, I make them wait and see.

During dinner a carafe slips from the butler's hand—wine and glass on the floor.

My father's one of the first to leave. He has a plane to catch to—I don't hear the name of his next resort. A month later he was dead in Majorca. During the farewells the girl's face is as veiled as mine—so similar, in fact, that he might notice the resemblance, which would never do, not now. Turning away, returning to my open door, I examine the jumble shop the water's become.

Just across the water you and I stayed. There. On the second floor. The room at the far end on the right. How we laughed when we ordered ham and eggs and got thin pink slices of meat on a bed of ice and egg salad. You're the only thing I ever saved. If a lady were to ask me I'd say love dwells in memory, moves in memory, is formed by memory, just as the evening light was formed in the curtains that screened it—but no lady asks.

CHAPTER II

*C*an't sleep tonight. I was lying in bed reading
the biography of a great man whose genius deserted him. Then I switched off the light and tried
to sleep, but I was afraid of something. I got up
and made scrambled eggs in the dark, standing
there naked and cold, watching the slime from the
bowl churn up into gray curds in the pan. They
looked like brains on the plate. I ate them and
they were delicious, perfumed with tarragon. I
poured myself a glass of milk and felt like a good
little boy, though the glare from the refrigerator
revealed that my body's no longer boyish—odd,
troubling reminder. Good boy in a man's body.

I sat by the window on a cold metal chair and
looked out at a black building across the way pressing its bulk against the wintry haze, which was
bright enough to suggest dawn, though surely that's
at least an hour away. The genius who deserted me
was you.

A psychiatrist I once knew told me that the unconscious, that irritating retard, can't distinguish between abandoning someone and being abandoned
by him. I guess he meant that even though I left
you, it's come to seem as though you left me. That
rings true. He also said that I was making myself

into a "quiet disaster" in order to force you into returning to save me—once again a dimwit stratagem hatched by the unconscious, which doesn't recognize any of the ordinary dimensions such as time, distance, causality or your indifference.

I never kept a diary. I never saved up witty things people told me. I never even bothered to remember my own past, the events that mattered most to me. Nor have I tried to piece things together. I'm a master of the art of pruning, you might say, as though I'd heard that plants should be cut back to make them flourish—except I keep hacking them down to the roots and wonder why they die.

Not all of them do. You're tenacious. Like a tree in paradise heavy with birds.

The leaves hang against the summer sky, real, not stirring, transected by the evening sun; the birds circle and light on its branches weightlessly. You know not to touch me, though I can sense you want to. We're both in jackets and ties, feeling formal after so many days on the beach in swimsuits. I can't be more than . . . twenty, but I look younger. Everyone says I do except you. You've learned to avoid describing me to myself, since everything you say provides me with another excuse to be vexed. It's a holiday and we've strung lanterns and put out flags along the walkway in honor of the occasion. The decorations, too, lend formality to the evening.

Belle comes toward us across the lawn, smiling, her nose and temples red with today's sunburn. Now she's dressed and has a cardigan over her shoulders. She kisses my cheek, as she did the first time we met, though this evening I catch her darting a glance in your direction the moment she pulls away. Have you told her we're having one of our little disagreements?

Over supper the Captain, the only man who looks natural wearing an ascot (his is yellow with age and the ends hang straight down in crumpled afterthought), neglects my glass and my remarks, which is not like him. And he brings up names I don't know but that you and Belle do. He's excluding me from your old circle, reminding me that there are dozens of people who have admired you for years—tribute-bearers assembled before the throne in their native regalia (gauze leggings over gold pants, woven-feather bodice above a hairless stomach, a short military skirt), their origins so exotic and the precise degree of their vassalage so old and various that only a historian could explain it—but the Captain explains nothing and you're invisible behind the incense rising from the bronze tripod.

All during the festival and the fireworks after supper I avoid you and stay with the Portuguese family who take care of your house. When you catch up with me and ask me where I've been, I say, "It's impolite for couples to stick together."

"Are we still a couple?" you ask.

"Maybe. You should know. You've known so many people whose names I can't even recognize—"

"I don't know *why* the Captain—"

"Why shouldn't he talk about anyone he wants to? Isn't it a little artificial to pretend I'm part of your old gang?"

As we walk out to the end of the dock, our feet sounding a different note on each slat of this crooked xylophone, your hands sketch out several possible replies, none to your satisfaction. From a distance we might look like a patriarch and his heir in our nice summer jackets, out for a stroll on a re-sort island. That's what a stranger would think. Your friends might say, "They've reconciled. Thank God we didn't let slip anything nasty about the boy while they were quarreling." We stare across the bay toward the lights of a town that rise in a curved band like the crown of a child coming toward us, candles in her hair to celebrate the festival.

The gleam of that bright town in the distance, in-tensified here and there where a car's headlights shoot out over the waves for a second, fills me with a longing to flee you.

Now, years later, how easy it is to interpret that urge as a loveless boy's fear of a perfect love that came too late, but back then it seemed (my longing to get away) almost metaphysical. In fact I said to you, as we stood on the dock, "Doesn't it ever strike you as strange to be a man rather than a woman, to be here rather than," pointing toward the crown of candles, "there, for instance? Some-times I want to explode into a million bits, all con-scious, and shoot through space and then, I don't know, rain down on everything or, well, yeah, actu-ally catch up with the light rays that bounced off people thousands of years ago. Somewhere out there," my lifted hand was pointing straight up, "Solomon is still threatening to cut the baby in half."

You turn silent and I'm afraid, once again, that

I'm boring you. Oh, now, my friend, I can see you loved my enthusiasm but didn't know what to say nor where to begin. So you looked away and I thought you were bored. The hot ingot I had become cooled and hardened.

"Shall we head back?" you asked.

"Go on," I said. "I'll stay in the beach house tonight. I want to play records very loud."

"You can do that—"

"*My* records. Anyway, I don't want to be anywhere near you tonight."

"Have I done something wrong?"

"Of course not," I said and looked you in the eye and smiled ever so brightly. I was so angry at you, but you climbed in my bedroom window and I relented.

Old friend, you studied me too closely, as though deeper scrutiny would finally reveal my mystery. But there was nothing more to learn, nothing definite in me beyond one surge of emotion after another, all alike and of the same substance, though this one broke early and fanned out timidly across the sand whereas that one broke late, right beside the reef, and shot spray up against the solicitous sky.

On the ferry the next day as we headed back toward the mainland and home, I was caught between regret for the difficult summer and anticipation of the fall. We all sat on the top deck under the sun and even the noisiest holiday-makers grew silent and breathed in the salt breeze.

Once we had docked in that surprisingly vernal inlet, the foliage to the west, where the sun had just set, was already black whereas the trees on the other side were still somberly green. Motionless up to the very moment of our arrival, the branches, once we landed, began to churn and revolve—rides in a somnolent amusement park that function only for the paying visitor. In the taxi to the train station we were jammed in with other vacationers, none of whom we knew, and I was happy to sit scrunched up beside you with one arm around your neck. But I didn't turn to look at you.

Back in the city I had more freedom than on the island, more freedom from the surveillance of your friends. You changed everything to please me. Took down the curtains, rolled up the rugs, stored furniture, painted every stick and surface white—I was in my stark, simple period. Now I've lived so long in hotels I can't imagine caring about my surroundings. They're things to accept, like people, not to change.

One night that fall I brought home a man I'd met during intermission at a theater. We, you and I, had an unspoken rule not against infidelities but against adventures that were conspicuous, intrusive. But nothing pleased and frightened me so much then as to cast aside all our rules.

I set up a little campsite in the kitchen for him and me, that is, I dragged in a brass lamp (one that could be dialed down to near extinction), a scratchy radio and a Chinese red blanket. I bolted the doors and that man and I became drunk and raucous. Once, near dawn, I thought I heard you pacing the hall. Cheap music, cheap wine, fumbling sex with someone who was homely, grateful, not even very

16

clean—what fun and anguish to defile the polished tiles of that kitchen floor beside the room where the maid slept. Just before she was due to awaken I saw my visitor out, though I prolonged the farewell by the front door, whispering and giggling. Lurching about I then restored the lamp to its proper place (my "study" as you called it), threw out the empty bottle and the cigarette ashes and cloaked myself in the red blanket. You were awake and dressed, sitting on the edge of our bed, talking and smiling but inwardly subdued and angry.

"Don't pretend with me!" I said, still drunk. "What are you really feeling?"

"Toward you?"

"Yes, of course, toward me."

You stood and looked out the window at the tree whose leaves were not coloring with autumn, just drying and curling. "This can't go on, can it?"

"What can't?" I wanted the full scene. "What can't go on?"

"I don't need to elaborate," you said and left the room.

The next day as I was walking my bicycle down the hall you stopped me at the door on your way in and invited me to dinner on the following evening. "Okay, maybe," I said casually. After all we lived together.

"Maybe?"

"All right!" I shouted. That was good, wasn't it? We needed to shout, didn't we? "Black tie? White tie? Shall I bring flowers?"

"Eight o'clock. Here." Only when I looked back did I see you watching me with the big brown eyes of a child—the child in a sailor suit you had been and whom I knew from that old photograph in the family album up at the cottage.

I had so much power over you. If I would touch you, as I did once in a while (just a touch, nothing intimate), you'd get excited. I could insist you cancel your social engagements for a week in a row and you would comply, but then that full, powerful life you led away from me would gush in through a crevice I'd neglected and inundate you and, yes, me as well. The telephone would ring, at a restaurant someone would stop by our table, people would drop in, on the street you'd be recognized and friends would draw us away.

You possessed a genius for friendship, a gift you'd refined through energy and intelligence. Your intuition was so keen that you could even sense when a shy person needed to be *ignored*. Yet there was nothing slavish about your politeness. You were cool and, among old friends at least, demanding not of favors, never favors, but of wit, if that means saying something interesting. I have not, now that you've left me, tried to imitate your style, nor could I; I'm simply carried about from place to place. When I was with you I did try to say interesting things from time to time. Not now. What I've learned is that people will get me home no matter how much I drink and pick me up no matter how little I said or offered the night before. As with possessions, I've given up conversation, but everything still goes on.

We gave a party in honor of an old musician visiting our city. The visit was only a pretext; we

18

scarcely knew the man. Hundreds of guests came.
Everyone wanted to meet him. We wanted, I suppose, to show your friends how much we loved each
other all over again. I stood at the door and shook
hands and told people where to put their coats.
Then I passed a tray, which I liked because it gave
me an excuse to keep moving. Finally I joined a
group and asked our guest of honor to tell me the
significance of the red thread in his lapel, and
people seemed pleased by the naiveté of my question and the modesty and humor of his answer.

But I couldn't keep it up. Suddenly I was tired
and even angry. I rushed to the back of the house
and sat on the sooty ledge of the storage room. A
few people found me in there and we had, after a
while, a band of renegades among the old cans of
paint and the tools and firewood. The renegades
agreed parties were a terrible bore and they drank
a lot and I was quite free to become silent and inch
still farther out the window. To me the atmosphere
seemed rebellious and one I alone had created. I
was very happy until someone asked me, ever so
casually, a question. She was a young woman in a
black gown. She had lovely breasts and diamonds in
her ear lobes, and she wasn't much taller or older
than I. "What's it like," she asked, "living with
him?" I could tell how much she admired you and
envied me. I tore off my tie and jumped off the
ledge into the alleyway and ran to the corner with a
cocktail shaker in my hand—silver and engraved
with your initials entwined in mine. I drank right
from the frosted spigot and tossed the empty
pitcher in a trash can, but only after I'd lit a match

to look at those initials incised in white metal. The engraver had worked cleverly; at first glance the design seemed to be a flourish in a scroll. The letters became apparent only after—ouch! I dropped the pitcher and it made a pathetic clang against the bottom of the trash can.

I ran and ran until I reached a promontory overlooking the city and the river. There I sat on a stone and stared at the cars below as they flowed across the bridge, their lights infusing the water like the blood of an antique senator in a tub. The cool moist earth tried to talk to me but it didn't have a mouth, just something through which it exhaled. Maybe it breathed through its pores. I took off all my clothes and clasped my skinny body, shivering. At my feet lay that little puddle of garments you had bought me. At last I was free of them, the dress shirt, the shoes and socks, the coat and trousers. I studied the watch and its black Roman numerals that circuited through its round ("I," "Aye, Aye!," "eye, eye, eye," "ivy") past the ecstatic shriek "VIII" and on to the dignified "X my sign." Now it was 1:30 and the hands said "I vie," as I did with you and your light yoke, your silk shackles. I threw the watch on top of the pile and strode away, still clutching myself, into a chilling fantasy of freedom. For a moment I had the illusion I was walking through a true forest until I came to a metal grille sunk into the ground through which I could see more cars streaking down a tunnel. The warmth and odor of the exhaust filtered up around me and I stood on that grating I know not how long. Could I pry it open and drop onto the shiny roof of a car, crawl to its hood, shrink and turn silver as the ornament breasting the wind? Or slip into a window, surprising a contented family, Dad vigilant and responsible behind the wheel, Mom reading a map by the faint glow of the open glove compartment, the kids and the collie a dim, dozing heap in the back seat?

If I said nothing they might take me home to a bungalow in a development and clothe me and keep me and you would never find me. They might consign me to the back seat and I, too, could become implicated in that tangle of fur, doggy breath, cool hands and cheeks as smooth as glazed fruit, our upturned eyes seeing only the tops of buildings, then trees, then after a while the stars and our ears catching only the murmur of grownups navigating us safely to our beds.

CHAPTER III

The answer to the riddle—what's preserved but moves? what existed only in the past but rustles, flickers brilliantly into sunlight, then soars?—is you, your presence, thoughts of you. Higher, into the sun, as hard to see as flight in white haze, then a swooping return to pounce, sharp-clawed and weighty, on my fist and to wriggle its head into the midnight confines of the leather bonnet, the instant ruff relaxing feather by feather back into a sleek neck, blindly turning to attend that snap of branches, those laughing voices beyond the hills.

Now I forget everything, and for some time I have practiced negligence and disorder. Yet you are everywhere beside me. Talking to someone about something as we start the morning's second bottle of wine, I lean back and close my eyes, studying oblivion, but my cigarette, which I'd forgotten in my hand, singes a few hairs, and the delicate sound, like silk tearing, awakens me to a recollection of you. On a beach. Red swimsuit and there a gull above us, prehistorically huge. A scramble over rocks, past a naked man in a moon-crater he's dug out for protection against the wind—I dismiss the thought. The singed hairs fall to my sleeve.

I used to say I came here because it's the one

place that meant nothing to us; my dramatic flight I kept fatuously (no, bravely) calling "the only gratuitous act of my life."

My indifference to this city was real enough, at least at first. Not knowing the language, I walked everywhere. I was afraid to take a bus; I didn't know which end to get on, or the routes, or how to pay. In all the city I had only one acquaintance, Didi. Her mother, a passionate anglophile, had made English the language of the nursery. The mother died when Didi was six. As a result she could say, "Don't dawdle," but had no words to express those obsessions collecting in her head like bad weather, turning the circles beneath her eyes ominously black and electrifying her hair.

Past the massive gates of her "palace," guarded by a man asleep behind smudged glass, into a mustard-colored atrium captioned with Latin inscriptions in relieved plaster and presided over by a rain-streaked goddess emblematic, undoubtedly, of one of the less lovely virtues (Prudence, perhaps); into the stairwell, filled if only questionably superseded by the narrow shaft of an elevator in which one person could stand, hear rattling chains and pray for ascent, as the "Virgin" might in an amateur passion play; and released into the dubious heaven of her apartment, I made my way day after day. My cheeks ached from smiling, my brain from combining and re-combining the fifty or sixty words I had learned. Next door, in her father's apartment, I'd sit beside the electric fire and watch the old man drag his body, broken at the hip and mended clumsily, from wall to wall, from the camp bed to the foul kitchen to a desk piled high with not current work but accumulated sloth; and he'd talk about Time. I have no mind for abstractions, never have. If someone speaks, as he did, of Time (in conjunction with "duration," "dimensionality," and "syncopation") and ends on the word *synthetic* (by which he means a process rather than a product), I sink into a swoon where Father Time hurls a slow-motion sickle out toward me, who am playing jazz on one of those featherweight pianos the Germans designed in the '30's for deluxe aerial travel. And if the discourse goes on, as the father's did, I rise from the aluminum piano stool and drift toward the concave bay window lined in bone-colored Bakelite, take a seat and, sipping Pernod, watch the massive bulk of our dirigible cast its shadow far, far below over foaming, sunstruck clouds. . . .

Didi and her father quarreled like lovers. He accused her of drinking too much, sulking inconsolably, scorning her painting and sleeping away the day. His accusations were as just as hers that he drank too much, slept too little and ruminated too long on the imponderables of Time. Although a flimsy partition was all that separated their quarters, they would go weeks without speaking—and then, when they did break the silence, it would be on telephones so close to the partition that their real voices, muffled by plaster, trailed their crackling transmission: echoes through that rumorous medium, Time, which he studied and we all wasted.

His theories and their arguments I must be reconstructing out of my later knowledge (always partial) of their language. In the beginning I could

24

only catch a phrase here and there, as though they were lunging in the dark at piñatas and I was grabbing the odd favor, its shape distinct in my hand but its function foreign to my understanding. After a spat with him she would lead me with dark glances back to her lair, to another, larger electric fire and a drafty room she had cleaned only so that it might stand in exemplary contrast to her father's squalor. At midnight (the hour *seemed* to be midnight, though it could have been considerably earlier or later; her father's poetry of Time had banished the prosaic clock), she rang the bar on the corner and soon a boy in a long apron would enter her door with two liters of white wine. When drunk again, I started mentally playing with my few words. She strode around the studio, muttering a poem she was composing, her first line inspired by a linguistic slip of mine that she had found, in her melodramatic way, "prophetic." I was trying to discover the words that would convey I was grateful for the evenings she had spent with me, but I knew I was a bore, I'd be back after I could speak with some fluency—when she stood still and whispered, "I love you."

That has always been a city of well-dressed men who stroll through formal parks, hand in jacket pocket, a silk square tumbling from the chest like a gigolo's excuse, beguiling but obviously studied. We strolled, Didi and I, past giant posters that forbade all other posters, and she offered me her arm, which I meekly took. My clothes were shabby, my hands trembling, my hair in need of a barber, my shoes large and white with rain stains, but I moved gratefully under the swaying, sequined umbrella of her protection, safe for the hour's promenade from those inquisitive male stares. I took those men so seriously—that one, rising splendidly from his sidewalk table and flinging coins with Jovian aplomb into the waiter's closing hand; or this one, gold chain glimmering under the thinnest voile shirt, glow-worm caught in a web, his black coat flipping artfully open to expose its red lining ("priest without, cardinal within")—but Didi dismisses them all as vapid exhibitionists. "Look at their tight pants. Some are fascists, some communists, but to me there is no difference. All cock and ass, cock-ass."

And this salty dismissal so perfectly expresses her sentiments that she keeps saying it over and over again, "Cock-ass, cock-ass." If a gold-haired diplomat at a dressy party chats me up, she darts a glance back and forth from his smile to my nod, my laugh to the manicured nail he raises to make a point, and I know that when he leaves she will mumble to his back flaring its muscles under the taut, English wool, "Cock-ass." Or if I introduce her to a new friend, one I have met on my own, she will look through his pile of talentless caricatures satirizing "personalities" in politics or show business, or listen to his fatuous memories of the good life of greed in Alexandria under Farouk—and stare at us in disbelief. "But he is completely stupid," she will tell me when we're alone. "You cannot spot a cockass, you are deceived by long lashes and ordinary good manners." She will lean over in her old sports car (which is redolent of leather and gasoline) and search out my reluctant gaze in the street light. "Did you like him?"

I will nod and she'll say, in her best English, "Poor lad." She half-stands in her seat and with one abrupt gesture folds the canvas top back into the trunk. A kick of gravel spun by rear wheels lends those faded and long-neglected words of the nursery ("poor lad") a new, stinging dash.

The city revolves above me as I rest my head on the leather cushion, which is cracked by age and the elements. Like the constellations spun by a slowly turning and twisting brass projector onto the faultless black planetarium dome, in the same way the glowing white facades of the city seem to stream forth from her little car, the restless, sputtering source of such slow, radiant motion. If I sat up and took notice I was reminded that only the dome's highest columns and upper stories had been cleaned and lit; the lower floors still hid behind centuries of soot and decay.

You and I picked our way through these old stones on a vacation years ago, marveling at the fact that someone had once kept peacocks here in the garden (now the portico of a church) and provided his lover, proclaimed a god, with a tepidarium lined with lapis lazuli (now only an oval pond dulled with the scum of breeding mosquitoes). We went to bed early, rose early and did our "archeology" (as you called it) seriously, zealously, books in hand. That city we toured and the one I lived in later seemed to be two different places. When we went there it must have been late spring; I recall azaleas, pink and white, hanging in pots from street lamps.

Now it was winter and on some nights cold rain lashed the palm trees, which looked like old chorus girls playing an empty house. We knew the classical city and the Christian city; this time, on my own, I've ignored monuments of every sort except as they lurch into view when Didi turns a corner and then fall backwards like toppling Goliaths stunned by the pebble the car hurls up behind us. You would disapprove, but then again disapproval is a form of concern—of intimacy. Maybe, even now you are disapproving.

When my apartment was destroyed by fire, or rather smoke, I found myself homeless in the street, face smudged with soot above, below, around my blue eyes; I must have resembled one of those peasants whom aristocrats two centuries ago would get up as Moors if a genuine black was beyond their means. I was glad to be rid of my falsely elegant quarters set down so incongruously in that folkloric district. Day after day I had sat behind sheer curtains, diaphanous in the light as love is the darkness drawn from night, where I heard rotund mothers bawl out the ancient names of their children. Imagine a fishwife screaming, "Psyche, come here. Eros, stop that!" and you will have some notion of the sounds I was attending in my dim seclusion. That was no place for a single man, a rich foreigner, a stray drone in an alien hive. I'd hear spasmodic creaking and look to see sheets and towels jerking on a line across the narrow street, or rather their shapes playing on my gauzed window—scalenes billowing into rhomboids or rectangles or twisting into broad-shouldered,

28

narrow-waisted shadow puppets projected on my screen, tormented penitents in white robes following a pink crescent and flying a mysterious red banner split into two streamers (a pair of girl's panties and the dangling arms of a scarlet shirt). The lady from the bar down the street sent me a glass of hot milk, her remedy for inhaled smoke, and two neighbors offered me a room in their apartment. Someone said Didi had probably started the fire (until now I had not known that she owned my building).

Free of all possessions, retaining only my black face and blue eyes, I moved like a specter through that city of well-dressed men, women, children. They fell back at my approach. Students, after leaping on a passing bus, looked at my charred progress; they swayed on the open platform, dresses and shirts fluttering, books dangling on leather straps like suspended disbelief.

Peter took me in. He confessed he needed someone to "help" with the rent. In fact, he was penniless, or had only enough money to buy breakfast every morning for himself and his black dog, Anxiety. Straining on her smart leash, as soft and slender as a woman's watchband, Anxiety would pull her proud, emaciated master down the five flights into the early spring sunlight. Thick blond hair straightened and coiffed under a blower, pale body dramatized by a well-brushed blue velvet suit, his great height further exaggerated by high heels, Peter strode to the corner bar, tossed back a thimbleful of bitter coffee in a single fashionable gulp and ordered two croissants. As he nibbled one, he slipped the other to Anxiety, who ate hers with moaning zeal; then she looked up with eyes either reproachful or sorrowful and unquestionably large, avid and golden. Peter brushed crumbs off the counter with a flick of his hand, and Anxiety snapped here, there, up, down and even looked over her shoulder for a vagrant morsel before yawning and sinking to the marble floor. She placed her cool black nose between her outstretched legs—an unsuccessful attempt to regain her dignity.

I fattened them both up. The rent, I learned, was months overdue; one night the lights went out; the next day the phone was dead. I paid the bills, hired a woman to clean and cook, and bought azaleas for the terrace. The one service no one could turn off was the endless flow of water. It poured out of a rusted pipe into a stone basin on the terrace. One side of the basin was sloped and ridged into a washboard, bearded with moss. Where the water originated and who paid for it no one knew. Its flow varied. One gray morning the terrace was flooded and stray cats picked their way across it, shaking their paws dry at every step. I longed for ballerinas to learn this *pas de l'eau*: tentative placement of the toe, slow balance, suddenly a flurry of rising beats.

There are some forms of love I guard against— the form Anxiety offered, for instance. Her devotion (slavish, greedy, forgiving) must be bad for the character of its recipient: mine, in this case. Spinoza warns us against lavishing the affection on pets we should reserve for other human beings. And yet I could not hold out against her. If I paused at the front door or absentmindedly fingered her chain dangling from its hook, she lowered her head then leapt up and started her awkward spins, tearing yaps out of the air as though it were fabric she were shredding. Or once, when Peter forgot to give her food, my sleep was troubled by the weight of a succubus, no—I was the patient, the doctor was passing an alcohol-cool disk of cotton over my neck and chest, the tray of instruments rumbled up, twin streams of warmed ether blew across my cheek . . . and I awakened to find a hungry Anxiety crouched imploringly on top of me, searching my face. Barefoot and groggy, I boiled her a few grams of noodles, the only thing in the cupboard.

Didi liked the dog, too, though in a blunter way more suitable to her communist style. They were comrades and Anxiety, hypocritical and ever adaptable, toned down her bourgeois effusiveness when we went for a ride or a walk with Didi. Across a glaring gravel park the three of us struggled in silence. A white male terrier joined our party and mounted Anxiety beside the crumbling temple of Fortune. Three pelvic thrusts and it was over—except the terrier could not pull free. He whimpered, returned his front paws to the ground, Anxiety cast sheepish looks at me—and still they were stuck and in pain. Two maids in black uniforms and white, starched aprons breathlessly ran up, shouting, "Fred, Fred," adding a final vowel to the name which sounded like "Frayed, Afraid." Anxious and afraid, this two-bodied monster limped under the immensity of an imperial arch. Every pictorial indication of perspective gave depth to the scene: the mid-afternoon shadows thrown by the running maids; the texture-grading of the gravel, receding from precision to blur; the converging lines of the broad avenue beyond the arch soaring smoothly to the horizon; the cool gray vagueness of the umbrella pines on distant hills; the tensing of ciliary muscles as my pupils accommodated the paired dogs in the foreground or focused on a soundless stone harp far, far away and sharpened the detail of each marble string but simultaneously lost, lost the present . . .

I'm wandering. When we lived together I devoted my nights to fleeing you. No need to go into all that, except I'm certain you saw those nights as wonderful orgies in unfurnished student rooms— drinks, drugs, casual sex (what you considered my father's immoral influence). Every night I was lowering myself farther down the rock face. I swung in the wind on ropes payed out by you, and each time I touched the sheer wall I blindly sought with my boot for a foothold, the slightest purchase. Nothing. Nothing.

And yet I couldn't resist demanding more line, looking farther down for that ledge or shelf I needed. Once it crossed my mind to cut the ropes and float free. Was I unworthy of the gift you'd offered? Had I summoned you with kabbala alone (the thousand readings of the letter Aleph that begins *Leviticus*) but not been ready for your coming? Now that I am ready you have hidden your face.

In those days I was not yet the ghost I've become. Awakening in the middle of the night I would hear the squeal of tires on asphalt or the voice of a midnight drunk beseeching our windows, and I would resent your peaceful sleep, the measured rise and fall of your chest, not because it was breathing away my youth (I'd be young forever!) but because you were the living barrier between me and the danger I didn't want to digest, only devour. I pictured where my clothes were and in my imagination collected them, put them on and escaped you with the startling ease of a time-lapse film of an opening flower, its modest green petals blushing faintly, then exploding into rays of fevered scarlet.

The actual preparations took longer and produced a considerably less colorful result. I bathed my face, neck and hands in a liquid bronzer and assembled a ragamuffin costume out of moth-eaten gray slacks from a thrift shop, a see-through rayon shirt as yellow as the applied bronzer, racing shoes topped by sagging wool socks, striped in blue, and a white silk jacket embroidered with a dragon. My appearance was composed out of allusions to things or people I admired—the slacks from an old gangster movie, the shoes and socks from the athletes I'd watched at school circling the track, the jacket from a veteran whom I'd studied once during a two-hour layover in a bus terminal, the gauzy shirt from a circus barker whose masculinity had become all the more pungent through dandyism. That nothing went together or suited me I suspected no more than that these invoked male presences, sinister and glamorous, were visible to my eye alone. Only now do I see that my own beauty outshone and redeemed those clothes, any clothes, and if I speak of my beauty I do so only because I've lost it.

My life of adventure was banal, of course—a ride in a stranger's jalopy to a distant neighborhood for a "party" that, after it fizzled, left me, the sole guest, venturing at dawn down a suburban street, curving mathematically past parked automobiles as the shaded windows hurled an orange sun from pane to pane. Or the crawl from one apartment to the next as the night train of young people in a big city lurched onto a dozing siderail or shuddered into hesitant motion or was switched from one track to another, routes changing as fast as warning lights could click from red to green or zebra bars could fall or rise. Here I am, drinking and sitting on a soiled couch in an empty room, explaining you to a black-haired girl with tiny features who keeps leaning another quarter-inch closer to me and gasping to indicate she's about to say something that never gets said because a fat man whose bald pate keeps his ringleted fringe well-oiled has come to escort me to an after-hours club where I dance with a man who purports to be the mayor's younger brother and knows of a livelier spot that turns out to be his room in a run-down boarding house where I watch him dust his swollen feet with lilac-scented talcum powder and listen to him bewail the loss of a lover whose heartless opportunism is immediately evident, though only to me. The tears, gin and powder drive me back out into the night and to a party at an address I find scribbled on a corner of an envelope. The guests have gone. The host is teetering down the hall as he puts out the last of the garbage, all bottles and ashes but he asks me in for a nightcap, though night, knocked out in the final round, is dying, and as its eyes go blue, its face white, body cold, a noisy throng of spectators rushes toward the superb corpse paling in the square ring. I suddenly want you. All the way home I cry and plan what I'll say, but I get no farther than "At last I've seen the light. Blame it on my youth," and these absurd words work their rhythm into my steps. While I head home in my tatty finery I breast a tide of commuters flowing up to engulf our island. You, above it all, puttering around the kitchen, are preparing eggs and tea; my fierce avowal cools under the glint of your glasses. I say something belligerent and go to bed.

I'm awakened for dinner and submit to the kindness of your friends. As the meal moves through its many courses and the conversation varies accordingly, my restlessness grows. Behind the ropes of music and talk the unknown giant stirs, props himself up on one elbow and shakes his head. He's still groggy but ready for another round. When he looks out at us and into the glare, he smiles hideously—the rubber guard has canceled his teeth.

I wanted nothing more than to flee those assembled saints and the mild glow you shed over us all (you were always good at lighting). The giant was on his feet again; someone had drenched his head with a bucket of water. He wipes his face with a towel. He is alert. He's ready.

I left your dinner party early and rushed downtown to meet the black-haired girl with the tiny features. She had a scheme that would make us rich—all we had to do was go to this address where her girlfriend Betty would place the crucial call to a contact she had who was on the best of terms with this bouncer in touch with . . .

Peter made me handsome again. At least handsome in the selfconscious style of that city. An Australian lady washed, cut and brushed my hair into a frozen wave, breaking on an angle above the fontanelle and surging over the left temporal lobe. I, too, was encased in blue velvet and white linen. My careful ties and careless handkerchiefs matched. Unpatterned, slender shoes, as soft as chocolate bars left in the sun, hats with rakish brims, a nearly hidden gold chain long enough to suggest the chest it plumbed, silk stockings and bikini underwear, pants without pockets—when Didi saw me she said, "But now you, too, are a cock-ass," and I knew I had succeeded.

Just as the most passionate cry, the most primitive outburst of sobs and shouts can be broken down into its phonemic elements and assigned to the speaker of a particular language, even a particular dialect, in the same way those nearly silent days under the orange awnings of restaurants and those revolving, spotlit nights could be categorized, if only retrospectively. For instance, the stalled, big-eyed emotional sequence that led to Didi's attempt to kill me. Or the foraging expeditions Peter and I went on after midnight: one night picking up the newsboy, a red-faced, uncircumcised peasant newly arrived from the South who was incapable of sustaining the formal *you;* another night climbing into the Mercedes of a Paraguayan we chatted with at three a.m. in the remotest section of the park; or the night after the national soccer victory seducing an excited lad without precious experience. Peter was still undressing when the trembling boy embraced me and exploded. As our guest slipped back into his underwear and lit the first of many cigarettes, he began what he called "the dialogue" by saying, pompously, "In principle it was dull." Peter had more of a taste for things of that sort than I, who retreated to another room and a jealous but exuberant Anxiety; "All is forgiven" her thumping tail signaled as she lay under the bed, concealed by the harem walls of the cotton spread. And then, at dawn, Peter joined us. He put down the half-empty bottle of vodka and told me he loved me. At noon he reached for the bottle when he awakened and we never left the house till dark. Or I could work out another sequence of the flirtations I failed to understand: Lily and her husband George, for instance, or the young baron studying Blake who confessed his love for me only when an unsuccessful film director insisted we play the "truth" game; or the sighs and unfinished sentences that the English girl favored me with when she brought the bank statements . . .

Now, I hear new versions of those stories that sometimes come clear, or threaten to. But if I am true to what I felt then and there, I must ignore gossip and avowals, since I was blind and deaf to them at the time.

To me there were comings and goings, congeries of bodies, faces floating up like thoughts out of ink. The long drive to the coast through the May fog in Didi's sputtering little car and supper in a deserted restaurant decorated with carved and painted crayfish. One party melting into another and the same opinions repeated again and again, as though conversation were being composed by the strictest serialist and, once determined, could only be inverted, transposed, or started from the middle. Another drive, this time with the Paraguayan up to a villa in the hills where an old American and his delicate Filipino lover were holding an "orgy." That night, as the Mercedes wriggled salmon-like up the curved road, I recognized that I was no longer afraid to die. Though I might draw back from a sudden threat, any prolonged one invited my indifference. We had drinks in the garden, then someone pulled me into a circle of dancers spiraling downward into the moist, hazy valley. Later I saw the Filipino in Peter's tight embrace as the two of them drunkenly rolled from one end of the room to the other. Every time the two-headed monster rolled past, the fox-trotting dancers stepped over them until finally they smacked into one wall with such force that the pier glass broke and shivered its silvery splinters to the floor. Peter and the boy were covered with odd-shaped bits of reflection—they were two continents (Europe and Asia, I suppose) wrestling under fragments of a disrupted Ocean; one piece of glass clinging to Peter's shoulder reflected my own somber eyes. After the lovers were pulled out of their dangerous rubble, they laughed—and ran up to the Princess bedroom where a racy member of the royal family was supposed to have spent a weekend with a commoner. The Paraguayan and I climbed a tree outside the

38

window and saw Peter raping the boy, who lay motionless and unaroused under the assault until Peter left the room for a second; then the Filipino began to masturbate energetically but with a frown, as though performing a routine yet irksome chore, or as though . . .

No more. No need to tell you that in the midst of my own adventures I would push back the body of the other man until I could see his face; for a moment I'd forgotten who he was. No need to tell you I argued with idiots about Verdi's place in the history of music. No need to tell you that one day I offered God the same prayer in eight churches.

Let me single out three images of children. The first was a French boy, no more than fifteen, who claimed he was walking to Paris on his way home from India. Certainly his feet were flat and blistered and dirty enough to lend substance to his tale. Peter and I bathed him and fed him. We took him to a movie, which he enjoyed. We bought him supper and a toothbrush. His skin was as soft and firm as yours, but his hair was different. The sun had bleached the outermost layer white but left the curls beneath a bamboo brown. That night he slept between us and called us his buddies; the next day he went down for cigarettes and never came back. The following day I threw his toothbrush away.

The second child was the six-year-old daughter of a German painter. She and her father and a group of intellectuals and I all drove in a caravan to a park of old stone monsters. While the others stayed behind at the gate under striped umbrellas and sipped Cokes and discussed political theory, the girl and I explored the grounds. Inside the mouth of a lion we sat on benches and she called out, listening for an echo that never came. As we were stepping over the weathered teeth she grabbed my hand— and I noticed that her nails were as smooth and clear as yours.

The third child I saw on an island in the South that belonged to Didi's family. For a week Didi and I stayed in her villa. Outside the windows were fat lemons on trees. The walls that followed the road to the sea were crushed under curtains of bougainvillaea. In the village we watched a woman and a band that had come over from the mainland present humorous songs in dialect under an arch of unfrosted light-bulbs. Didi and I thought we were the only foreigners on the entire island until one day we rode bicycles down to the harbor for lunch. There a yacht was moored, its teak gleaming and its mast tick-tocking like a discreet metronome. In the restaurant twenty men and women, the crew, sat at one long table. After days of seeing nothing but the dour faces and black dresses of the island women, I was blinded by these visitors from the capital with their splendid colors, coiffures, manners, jangling bracelets, loud voices. Didi muttered, "Cock-ass," but I could not stop staring at the gold filaments, silk scarves, the imperious examination of the fish stew, the charged exchange of glances after someone's insinuating remark, the whoops of laughter, the obligatory if languid political discussion. I looked up at them with wonder, like Neptune awakened by the swift keel of the *Argo*. Fools, yes. A pampered, ill-natured lot, to be sure. And yet they were as fascinating as a swarm of butterflies descending on a particular old tree, the thousands of bright wings pivoting on black bark. In their midst sat the only child, a boy in a sailor suit with eyes as large and serious as yours.

CHAPTER IV

Gregory of Nyssa, a fourth-century rogue (and brother of St. Macrina) whose first book extolled virginity, though he himself was never able to attain to celibacy for even a single day, hoodwinked the faithful with continual exegeses of that amoral hymn to voluptuousness, *The Song of Songs.* For instance, in Solomon's verse a randy girl exclaims with thigh-rubbing delight: "While the king sitteth at his table, my spikenard sendeth forth the smell thereof. A bundle of myrrh is my well-beloved unto me; he shall lie all night betwixt my breasts." The frank lust of a teenager bored at dinner ("Will these guys never stop talking?") but intoxicated by the douse of cheap scent she has too liberally applied to her wine-warmed flesh on the naive theory that more is more and half in a swoon as she elaborates a daydream about her own present attractions and those coming, tonight's experimental romp with him ("Let *me* be on top") and the lyrical aftermath, his sleeping head nestling between her beard-rouged breasts—this passage Gregory, after privately savoring, publicly interprets in these edifying terms: "There are many different perfumes, not all equally fragrant, from which a certain harmonious and artistic blend produces a very special kind of unguent called spikenard. . . . And so when the bride says to the bridegroom, 'My spikenard sendeth forth the smell thereof,' this is the profound lesson I think she is teaching us. It is that even though one may gather from all the different meadows of virtue every perfume and every flower of fragrance, and should make his whole life fragrant with the good odor of all these virtuous actions, and become perfect in this way, even then he would not be able to look steadily upon the Word of God, no more than he could the sun."

Why do I copy out this passage for you? Not to make fun of the worthy Cappadocian who lingered over his Old Testament lovers, returning to them again and again that he might explicate a sensuality determined not to be a mystery, a languor resisting interpretation if little else. No, I simply want to anticipate your laughter at *my* method, which will be his. For I, too, will relish an amorous history, then lift a hand from the page or my pleasure and find in vivid scenes portents.

Were any of those perfumes in that "artistic" blend drawn from the flowers I lived among, knew well but cannot name? Oh, some names I know: honeysuckle on the vine at the top of the tarred drive. Once past that black intrusion into our fields, that pungent strip that boiled in summer but cracked and hardened in winter, I reach, or rather return, to blossoms, some white, others yellow, all a muted, delicious release of scent, as though the inquisitive child had cracked open, silently as possible, a drawer in his grandmother's room, one filled with the decent, sexless things of a woman age has restored to innocence, among which glimmers a white satin sachet, the plump square packet trimmed in blue silk and a tiny, crushed bow. The satin yellows, as do the flowers, but unlike them it cannot be opened. I nip the green button at the base of a picked blossom and pull out the glossy stamen whose honey I strain off with my lips. The old-fashioned charm of the vine attracts bees as dowagers madden impoverished young men.

The path a hop over the fence led downwards into a valley slimy with leaves fermenting into a ceremonial liquor, past roots swelling up out of the ground like arms and shoulders (biceps bulged, triceps grooved, trapezoids pumped up into thick, twisted musculature): emergent wrestlers. Downwards on a route whose turns must have been imprinted on my brain during the first year of life, so well do I follow them even now, a route ending at a brook. There it is, shuttling like a brand-new power loom bright with spindles of light, bobbins of water, working at top speed. The current is broken by a stick, but just downstream from it the parted threads rush back over each other, ply of sun over ply of shadow. Before the water glides under the bridge it calms down.

Halfway up the path my collie, Tim, has stopped. Ears up and nostrils working, he burrows into the damp soil with the fanaticism of a miser unearthing his gold. But then, like me, he pulls free of his obsession as quickly as he entered it and comes trotting down to my side, a smile on his black lips and a pleasant, even a vacant sense of well-being in his eyes. He glances at the water with no interest; surveying its flow is a whim of mine he respects but does not share. He sits and lifts his face into a gust of wind, squinting. Then we're off again and he's a merry Sancho Panza beside my gloomy Quixote.

Next to a crude plant that hugs the ground, its big leaves as dry and cracked as elephant hide, lies a candy wrapper. As I pick it up, its wet cardboard tray goes soft in my hand. All I'm left with is the cellophane window, spangled with rain but still serviceable as glasses. Through them the brilliant day dulls and warps—until I throw them aside and plunge deeper into the valley. We chance upon—no, not chance, since I know every inch of these sacred precincts, better to say we return, with the solemnity of pilgrims, to a clearing and the shrine it encircles: a rusted ice box.

The autumn sun steams the long grass, broken and brown and sweet to smell. Tim settles down in its coarse strands, the better to point up the silkiness of his caramel-colored flanks. His lack of reserve before the felled deity (its wooden locker doors ajar and bleached, cold chambers hot, the ice compartment itself invaded by dandelions) annoys me, and I hold his muzzle shut and catechize him, as my mother lectures me hour after hour. I'm whispering in a flossy ear adorned with a dark brown burr, the closed lotus shape of its hull outfitted with bristles hooked at the ends like crochet needles or the Pope's crook. His eyes express sincere repentance, but a moment later he's smiling again, glancing complacently around at the congregation and up to the great rose windows of the trees, their leaves suddenly still and brightened. He yawns, he sinks his head into its luxurious fur ruff, he rests his snow-white chin on a beige glove, the pose intended to convey pious concentration but in fact a disguise for daydreaming. And yet his lack of fervor does not preclude a saintly gift for loving me—not the rigid, braced, *willed* love of lesser creatures, but rather the easy knack of sleeping when I sleep, waking when I wake, pacing on hard nails across linoleum when I suffer—the knack of having love as first nature.

The frost reworked the outdoors in a new medium: diamond splinters. The maids were still in their attic rooms; the house was silent except for the sound behind closed doors of my rabbit thumping up and down the back stairs (the vigorous ascent, the tentative, fearful descent); some couturier had thrown his creations all over the downstairs, a yellow scarf of sunlight tossed on the kitchen table, a red, narrow belt stretched taut on the pantry floor, shadow-blue gowns heaped high in the dining room chairs—and Tim and I slipped out into the jeweler's workshop. There, on the lawn, was my father passed out cold in his car, black tie undone, his shirt front pulled free of its black and gold studs and buckling to reveal an arc of lean chest, frost tipping his eyebrows, rhythmical puffs of breath visible in the air as I bent down to kiss his lips, foul with last night's alcohol. His cheeks were as rosy as mine.

All through that long winter Tim and I kept to the woods. When the rabbit died we attempted to dig him a grave but the ground was too hard. Our property was an odd remnant of another era, for it was surrounded by slums; just beyond the walls were streets, cars, trolleys, unpainted shacks pressed up against each other, the children leaning out windows or spilling down stoops—all glimpsed from the recesses of our car as it headed toward opening gates. Safe again, I sat up and saw the path under snow where violets would grow again next spring; concealed behind that low-gabled house (gingerbread crumbling under too much icing) is the frozen lily pond. And over there is my mother's stable. At night the world beyond the gates would penetrate the world within, and in the valley I'd hear boys hallooing to one another—the "bad boys" as my nurse Anna called them. She herself seemed not altogether good since on Thursdays, her day off, she'd spend the afternoons dressing for a visit to the dim, dangerous city outside. I'd hang around her tiny attic room, its ceiling sloped and smelling of copper and electricity. She kept singing "Ain't Misbehavin'," which I heard and repeated as "Ain't Mr. Haven." Sprawling on her chenille bedspread, I watched her wave her hair, dangle amethysts from her ears, step behind a screen, rustle and emerge in mother's last year's shantung dress. For a treat she'd dab her perfume, an unpleasant, synthetic lily-of-the-valley, on my wrists and slip a purple, licorice-flavored pastille between my lips. Her own mouth she'd redraw in red gloss, her new upper lip larger and wetter and more curved than the one I saw six mornings out of seven pressed to the white rim of a cup below eyes the color of coffee at the moment the cream surfaces. Tim and I, wandering through the woods moments before nightfall, heard city noises from over the wall and the warm, insinuating chuckle of a man—Mr. Haven, no doubt, waiting for an Anna who, despite a song to the contrary, would be his tonight. Crashing through the woods came my mother on Jasper, foam frozen on his bit, burrs on his withers.

When my father left us, I sat in my bed, holding my knees, listening to my mother's screams. Beside me Tim lay on the floor but kept one eye trained on me. I held a marionette in my lap and tried unsuccessfully to untangle the strings. When the howling and bellowing became too loud, I locked myself in the bathroom with Tim, but he's too excited by our novel hideout to grasp the seriousness of the problem—the problem, that is, of untangling Columbine. In the morning I found all the mirrors broken, the windows in the french doors painted black, sunlight eerily orange through the still-wet brushstrokes, in the basement the stench and rubble of her burned clothes and furs, on the back steps (no longer the rabbit's lair) a hammer beside jewels, some smashed to dust, others only cracked out of their gold or silver or platinum settings, and in the stable all three horses shorn of their manes, Jasper's neck shivering and raw. In the hay lay my mother, wide awake and silent, her hands bleeding. Columbine, at last, was dancing freely, and Tim and I invited the marionette to the ice box where she took part in the service.

Because the past came first it's old, deserted, a cast-away household fixture rusting in spears of grass that are as squeaky, now it's spring again, as washed hair. Out of the wreckage of adult passion,

diamonds pounded into dust; out of Mr. Haven's
chuckle and the face of a stranger illuminated in
match-light; out of leaf-mold and the arms and
shoulders of tree roots or men—from these scatter-
ings I fashion you.

When I left you (or you left me), I came bound-
ing into your study with my arm around Robert—or
rather with my hand reaching toward his shoulder,
since he was six-four. During that long last winter
with you I had kept searching for an excuse to
move out. Now I'd produced one: Robert. That's
not exactly true. I wanted to stay, I wanted to go, I
wanted to hide curled up within your hands, I
wanted to snap you in half and cast you aside.
Sometimes I simply wanted a response from you,
little understanding that I had it, moment by moment, though it was a tune played too softly for me
to catch, so softly it irritated me.

"This must be Robert," you said, rising and shaking his hand. Robert yawned (he was nervous) and I
don't think any of my descriptions of you (I could
talk of nothing else to him) had prepared him for
your actual presence. So much thought (not just
yours but your parents' and grandparents') had
gone into the way you handled an occasion that no
one as simple as Robert stood a chance. I was so
proud of you just then, surrounded as you were by
your books and paintings and the three photographs of me in a single frame, pictures taken in
this very room one afternoon. In the photographs I
could see the paintings and in one of them your
hand; the fingers were held as though you'd just
plucked a harp string—your equivalent to a shrug.

In the top photograph I was staring into the sunlight, my lips parted to speak; in the middle one I had tilted my head to one side to write something; in the bottom one I had twisted my body around and propped my chin on my fist. I was smiling in profile and the three smile lines beside my mouth were echoed in the folds falling from the shoulder of my white shirt—the lines, too, seemed to be smiling.

In his jeans and newsboy cap Robert looked absurd beside you. He had grown too tall. You invited him to join us for tea; I don't think Robert knew that "tea" could be a meal and the maid in her apron, he later told me, had seemed like a joke, something out of the movies. Clever move on your part, that tea, for I fell into my half of the ritual. I poured while you buttered things and the clattering and tinkling and stirring and passing left Robert speechless. Since I had already complained to Robert about how "grand" you could be, I was delighted to show you off at your most oppressive and even more thrilled to demonstrate my perfect familiarity with the despised formalities.

"How nice finally to meet you," you said. Robert took off his cap. In bars or on the streets everyone stared longingly after Robert; after all he did have blond hair, a brick-red face, great height and yard-wide shoulders. But here he seemed the delivery boy asked to "stay on" for a bit of cheer at Christmas time. Fortunately he had the wit or thoughtlessness to grab my thigh as I walked past on my way to the kitchen for more hot water. He pulled me down beside him and kissed me. For a second I tensed (you'd never actually seen me in another man's arms) but when I glanced in your direction I saw you were contemplating your cup, and that enraged me.

"I hate to say this," I began, "but I guess I'm moving out." My words made me as giddy and fearful as those times when my mother would pull up in front of my grade school and announce that she was whisking me off somewhere halfway around the world for a vacation. My notebook and the assignment I had been worrying about turned irrelevant, like a child's savings placed beside his father's millions.

"Oh?" you said.

"Yes. I've been so torn. But well, Robert's my age and I love him and he loves me and that's . . . though we're broke and he's only got a studio . . . "

"I don't want you to be broke," you said. "Just now you think you don't want any reminder of me, least of all money, but you're used to it and after a while you'll probably want some." You paused. "Nothing spoils love so quickly as poverty. You should give yourselves a real chance."

"How kind of you," I said sarcastically. "Thanks for the offer. But you're right. I don't want a reminder."

"Unless it's coming to you," Robert, ever practical, threw in.

Sometimes, my love, I wish I had refused the money then and later; as it's turned out, you've always owned me. Fearing that Robert might dilate on the subject of my dowry, I said, "Leaving you is really hard. It's been a hard decision."

51

You smiled politely.

"After all you've done for me." I turned to Robert. "I told you how he saved me from my father."

"Yeah," Robert said.

"Look," you said. You were standing. "No reason to prolong this . . . interview. When will you be moving?"

"Tonight."

Placed into the heavy pages of my childhood memories are photographs, some faded, others mutilated, some shot out of focus, others blurred from the first by subjects in motion: all of men. Few of the pictures were captioned at the time and I forget names. In every case the years have mercifully airbrushed out the ludicrous styles of another era, the baggy clothes and the haircuts (a line of white scalp dividing comb-carded designs preserved in oil; lather and razor throwing the ears into pitiless relief; clippers shearing the nape of its modesty or glory) and my past is continually updated, becoming as disheveled or tidy as this year's fashions might demand.

Here's one, the first in the book: a giant in khaki takes me onto his lap and gives me a pair of gold wings from his lapel. He pierces the frail strap of my sunsuit with the grooved pin and screws the round, notched clasp in place. Would an ordinary boy have thanked him then, slid off his lap and run off to play? I remain where I am. Above me he is talking to my mother, his low voice resonating through his body and into mine, awakening a string of overtones in me, each of his words a pebble skipping over the still water I've become, up through my legs, across my pale chest, sinking deep into my mind, where the rings are still widening. As his adam's apple works, I want to touch its rise and fall. Somewhere behind me my mother is murmuring responses. For the moment she is cinched tightly into the polite form of that time and society, but if he doesn't leave soon she will explode out of her stays and grow bigger, louder, angrier. The man doesn't sense the danger. We didn't know him very well, I suppose (now I don't know him at all except in the buzzing tympanum of my stomach, the tuning fork of my clavicle, the great cracked bell of my head).

But it is his very size—beneath, beside, above me—that makes my pulse throb and my stomach sink. Let this man be the well I drown in until I can no longer hear my mother's exasperation. Falling, falling though poised motionless on his knee, I hurtle into an infernal paradise at once terrifying and calm, inverted flames dripping into crystal lights. Let him kiss me with the kisses of his mouth.

When I was a teenager—oh my love, don't fear, I won't read off a Leporello's list of infant conquests, the constant inquests of evenings, troubled nights, the wan dawns of Don Juans. I have no desire to confess what you have already forgiven. Nor will I bore you by drawing out (as some anatomical charts transform for the sake of clarity the stomach into a long, neatly labeled ribbon) a tale that lies coiled, messy but alive, in the hot hollows of memory. Take your stick and poke the steaming entrails. Read them; read me.

I'm with someone's deb daughter, a girl whose perkiness seems calculated to please adults alone and whose interest in me is as exhausted as mine in her no matter how tirelessly she flogs her attention into new spasms of smiles, questions, compliments—but then she suggests we visit a certain Tom (that wasn't his name: I forget names). Tom, she tells me, is a lonely guy, not because people shun him, heck no, anything but, he's so darned attractive—just a loner, I guess. And should we visit him?

We should.

It's a June night, midway through the short social season, and Midge (we'll call her that) and I are leaving a "theme" party, some ghastly rodeo affair. I'm wearing the costume, jeans, a checked shirt, and as my rear-view mirror reveals a few wisps of hay in my hair. How we got to Tom's house, through it and then to the pool I don't recall, but what is happening now is his step up onto the diving board, his pause, and then his slow stride and the bounce up into the night sky, where he clasps his knees, somersaults—and remains, dark pine trees all around the blazing sapphire pool. Lit from below, he hangs in the brilliance welling up to his tensed legs and to his head ducked so far down between his knees that only his black nape, water-smoothed, is visible. His throat is as bright ivory overlaid with sapphire.

Who is this who comes out of the past like pillars

of smoke? A lifeguard, whose preposterous name I do happen to remember but will not give away. He is fascinated by me. At least he stares at me in nervous bursts from his lookout tower or when he descends and strolls to the water's edge, casual, lanky, but blowing imperiously on his whistle at a swimmer whose daring has over-reached his skill, or when he parades past my towel, golden hair aglow on his powerful legs. Back on his towel, nose, cheekbones and temples fierce with white war paint, he scans the beach—and stops at me. I lie like a crucifix between two swelling breasts of sand, the innocent dying between thieves. Then I prop up my chin on gritty hands and return his glance. With stealth and patience, after days of waiting, I find a moment to talk to him and something neutral to say. Surveying us are the glittering windows of my mother's seaside house.

One evening a storm blows up. The last swimmers have long since gone, including the cheerful coed whom the guard usually talks to (once, on a slow day made still slower by his embrace, the guard had lain beside her and in the bagginess of his swimsuit I detected one loose fold harden). She's gone. The guard and I are alone below mother's windows, each old pane set at a slightly different angle to reflect another segment of the darkening sky, seven hundred versions of a fractured pastoral, the trees sweating black honey, the clouds weeping nymphs and the waves tame animals grown wild.

The guard invites me into his narrow tower to escape the rain and closes the door. He's facing me. Out of the corner of my eye I see a shelf of first-aid supplies, a coil of rope, clear mosquito repellant and white sun repellant, an unstrapped watch, his painted nose and mouth, his gleaming chest, a stiffening fold, intricate knees, foreshortened calves still bristling gold into the gloom, one flexed to throw his body into relief and mine into confusion; on my lips I feel a coolness concealing warmth, amber over roses, just as the fragrance of coconut oil disguises the odor of sweat, just as his arm reaches out to encircle me. Someone's outside: mother, hooded, standing in the downpour. She drags me home. Her nails press a bracelet of pain into my tan wrist. As she looks on, I gaze into the mirror and with agonizing slowness wipe away the traces of lead-white paint from my mouth.

Turn the pages, beating them back faster and faster. An Indian, on his break at last, rises from the piano and leads me out of the bar to the end of the pier. We sit on the bench. He takes my hand. With the help of my bilingual dictionary, rich in claret leather, he haltingly assembles a plan for our escape—tomorrow night, the boat expectant under a gardenia moon gone yellow, and then a plunge through parting spray to a village where his mother, at first as wooden as his devotion, then as efficient as my beauty, awaits us on the white beach, her shoulders wrapped in a pink, stirring rebozo— but the dictionary is too rudimentary to give him all the words he needs ("my devotion," "your beauty . . . dollars . . . youth"). The Bible paper whirrs and crinkles under his moistened index finger. For some reason I look around and see my father sauntering out toward us, drunkenly smiling at the tropical stars, undoubtedly searching for the Southern Cross. "Daddy," I say, rising with magnificent aplomb, "I'd like you to meet a friend of mine. Pablo. Yes, Pablo. This is Daddy."

"Back to bed, son. Off you go. Pablo, how about a jazz rendition of 'Smoke Gets In Your Eyes'?" My father masterfully guides the poor man back to the bar. Come, my beloved, let us go forth into the field; let us lodge in the villages. In my troubled sleep the soft tread of an opera pump shatters the gardenia. The petals fall on the rebozo which, weighted, slides away to expose the relics of a child-sized saint, all bones and brocade within the flyblown glass case.

Like Isis, I fly up and down this long river, my brother, searching for the parts of your broken body that I might piece it together again, put the heart in your chest, wrap the mangled remains in linen and fan it back into life with my wings. In three children I have found your touch, your nails, your eyes. Your sex eludes me—have the fish eaten it? And shall I copy it from memory in wax and spices or in words? My falling tears swell the river as I hide in the papyrus.

Without names or dates, without records or traditions, how can I document what happened so long ago, far upstream where the river is barely a brook and a twig suffices to disturb its current? Tim and I are playing beside the brook, now or a hundred years ago. My mother has retreated into her wing of the old, sprawling summer house. At night a man lays a fire in one room and I stretch out in front of it, my nose buried in Timmy's fur, which smells of crushed grass. The fire pops as a pocket of trapped gas hisses into a yellow flare or a pine cone vaporizes into blue, spiritual flame, hard wooden petals opening and furling back into ash. In the miniature birchbark teepee beside me a still smaller cone of pink incense threads its pine scent through the pinhole at the top. When I lift the cover there stands a sagging gray replica of the cone—which one breath disperses. This time I select green incense and watch its shiny point stubbornly resist the match's torture and then, just before my fingers are burned, the sinner smoulders, repents, exhales a whispered confession of heresies more satanic than we had dared suspect. Absolved and saved, the happy victim burns to the ground.

No one beside the man who does chores will come near us. I haven't seen mother in days. At night, now, I can hear her drag furniture from one end of her room to the other, or it could be the steamer trunk. One morning I found her black wool bathing suit flung over a couch. I lifted it, wet straps brushing my arms, and breathed in the smell.

That was a museum of other summers, of lost pastimes. Here is the Chinese checkerboard, colorful rays pocked with empty sockets—it's lost its marbles. And here the slack hunting bow that, when it was taut, only my father was strong enough to draw; beside it a leather quiver of arrows, backswept feathers dry and split though the metal tips remain lethally sharp. Up the uncarpeted cedar stairs and to the left, then to the left again, take a right: the playroom, its linoleum floor printed with a blue and green picture of the globe. I take a step toward the South Pole, change my mind and pace up Africa, stop on Italy, my shoes swiveling on its boot, amble over Asia and kneel on the apoplectic face of the East Wind to search out a book, my favorite, the story of a spinster toad in bonnet and gingham skirt notorious for her nasty behavior toward the good-natured frogs. And here's another, a tale of a benign elephant family wise to the point of sadness, reconciled to the humiliations of a long life but gifted with a naive delight in travel—in the pranks, say, of their foreign host and friend, a monkey. The infinite sadness of the elephants in their railroad coach! They're arrayed in old-fashioned clothes and waiting with dignity at the end of the book for the beginning of yet another holiday. They have assumed an expression of mild curiosity for want of any more avid hankering after adventure. Thoroughly enlightened, detached yet compassionate, the elephants are impersonating an ordinary family, though for them the steamer trunks, the wicker hampers, the matching valises, the plush seats steeped in coal smoke, the net hammock bulging with still other impediments—all these barricades against the flames and rapids beyond have paled into mere pencil sketches on transparent rice paper through which the elephants gaze unblinkingly, gay and courageous, at the devouring fire and water of transience.

I am not resigned. Like my mother I pace through the resonant house. I'm expecting someone. Out onto the lawn I creep, small under the moon. I'm alone, the only child outdoors in a slumbering village of old houses. Bending over the artesian well I press my lips to its cold flow that jets straight up and holds a constant dome night and day, as smooth and unflawed as sherbet from the scoop. The force of its driving current burns my lips. My mouth, shocked, only now warms to the taste of the water, a suspicion of iron as faint as the trace of pears in a liqueur that seems all clear alcohol, the pears more conspicuous on the label than in the liquid.

A rust-stained canvas lawn chair, its wood arms and legs the youthful bones emerging through old skin; the burrows of black earth turned back by moles; the two half-moon bridges over the pebbled bed of the brook, their curved rails and upright stangs leprous with matte wood and weathered varnish; the unlatched door of the woodshed and the bolted door of the narrow stall that houses the gas tank; the porch with its sun-faded straw rugs and creaking swing; the frog-loud grasses and mossy stones where the brook swells just before it fans out over glassy sand into the lake; my mother's windows, curtained to contain the burning lights—this whole realm the moon articulates with the precision of the fish man boning a mullet with a black knife under a running faucet, severing the head and tail, folding back the filets, nicking the tender flesh here, there, then lifting an unbroken tree of ribs branching out from a pearly spine.

I am waiting for someone. Back in my room I dry my muddy feet in Tim's warm ruff, then slip under the sheets and pull up the spread printed with dolphins soaring out of waves. My waiting has made me tense to every sound. Are those the wheels of his Silver Cloud crunching the gravel as he glides up the drive? Does the birch outside my window tremble in the wind or under his weight? In my daydreams he hops lightly over the sill into my room and I rise to greet him. Then the hurried escape into the night, the back door left open, Tim as ready to go as I; the brake is released, the car rolls down the hill without lights or power; when we reach the gates the starter button is pushed, twin beams strafe the post office, the grocery, the penny candy store, the raised gates at the railroad crossing and the forest beyond. Only now, still in my pajamas, do I steal my first glance at him. Tim discreetly settles himself on the floor between us and pretends to doze. Our headlights catch a distant road sign that rushes toward us; just as its letters fill the windscreen I read its warning: The End.

In a book of magic I've filched from my mother's sewing room I find spells to cause death to all the fish in a pond, stir up a quarrel at table, induce courtesy, cause the appearance of little people, diagnose virginity, know a woman's intimate secrets (two methods), destroy a faithless husband. One recipe intrigues me. Pour oil from a white lily into a crystal goblet, recite the 137th Psalm over the cup, then say the name of the planetary angel of Venus, Anael, then the name of the person that you love. Anoint your eyebrows with the oil. Touch the right hand of the beloved at dawn on the Friday following the new moon. Where can I find a lily? Whose name? And his hand is beyond my grasp.

I awaken to find Tim gone. He has deserted the oval rug beside my bed. Hurrying from room to room I call his name. I stop dead center in the playroom, a colossus bestriding the Atlantic, one foot on France and the other on Canada, but not even in the most distant recesses of the house can I hear the approaching clatter of hard nails on hard wood. He's back in my room, I'm certain of it. But there I see only a tuft of white haze from his belly floating over the rug. Afraid that one of my spells might have miniaturized him, I throw back the spread of waves and dolphins, but even in the white water of my sheets he's nowhere to be found, a tiny collie paddling through that dream-tormented sea. Is he in the sewing room, paws up on the window ledge, bird-watching? No. My mother's door is half-open. When I peek in, I see everything is impeccable; the accumulation of dishes has been removed, the bed is made, the curtains flung back, the floor swept. Her long suffering is over. The maids will return; she will make me blueberry muffins in the wood-burning oven; now I can be noisy again; we'll go for swims together; we'll go to the country club Sunday suppers; in the morning she'll tie up her hair in a scarf and, after I pole the ancient Chris-Craft out of the boathouse, we'll skim the lake, waving to friends on the beach; she'll sew; grownups will come by for drinks; she'll smile and ask questions and invite guests to stay on for dinner; the phone will ring—but where is she? Where has she gone? I search for her and Timmy everywhere, downstairs where I expect to find her with the newspaper and cold coffee in the breakfast room, on the beach as she emerges glistening from the water, in the garage, lifting the croquet set, rusted wickets dangling from the stand beside upright mallets and pocketed balls jiggling in their sockets . . .

I've wandered so far from my subject, my dear, which is you. You are the song I wanted to sing, the god I wanted to celebrate or conjure. Before I knew you I loved you, now you've gone I find you everywhere, and for me you are my past, present and future, unchanged, equivalent only to yourself, just as in that long poem of triple rhymes, each line ending in an echo natural but ingenious, there is one single word that admits of no variation, that Dante rhymed only with itself: Christ. Somehow I've lost the design of these pages. Whereas I wanted to trace you in my past, demonstrate the ways in which experience prepared me for you, all the while skipping the things that were painful or ugly—oh, I wanted to fashion, even falsify, a lovely story for your entertainment, but that house, that woman, that summer have entranced me. I was a juggler tossing my oranges in the thick air, my little skill my only gift, but bad memories have frozen my hand and fixed my eyes and the offering—not the fruit but its flying motion—has failed. The bells will not ring. This is not you, no, rather it is gold pierced through the fabric of my infant shirt. Gold? No. A ribald song that seems to flirt with night as Mr. Haven grows more bold. Song? No. A frozen leap tucked in a fold of sapphire sky, a dive transfixed, inert. Dive? No. White kisses on my lips, which hurt as I erase the tale the mirror told. For were you gold, I'd have you in my hand. If song, your harmonies I'd still command. A dive cannot be held in bright suspense. Kiss? No. Because your touch I can't erase. Yet I shall list for you my recompense. Gold, songs, a dive, a kiss—recall your face, perhaps, but you elude me still. I'm on your trail, but you elude me. Take my hand as with the other I open the latch to the garage door and swing it open.

The car motor is running and the garage is filled with exhaust. Coughing, frightened, I draw back, but after the fumes clear I approach the station wagon and look in—an old Town and Country, one of those station wagons with blond wood paneling on the doors. Behind the wheel is my mother, jaunty in her leopard-skin coat and matching turban and gloves. She's dead. So is Timmy beside her. I'll hang my harp on the willow.

CHAPTER V

Craig and I spent so much time at the theater that finally we began to live there. Moving in wasn't a decision (at least not on my part); to decide anything would have required a moment when I stood outside events or peered down at them all floodlit from the pinrail—and no moment like that came along. We brushed our teeth and washed out our underwear in a sink off the star's dressing room. For clothes we had the whole costume collection to work our way through, though Craig kept the building so warm that we could stroll around it naked. We ended up sleeping naked onstage in a hammock slung between two coconut palms, our bodies entwined like yang and yin, pang and sin.

Sunsets in the tropics are conveniently quick, a fast fade on the master dimmer, one smooth continuous descent of a shadowy hand on the rubber grip. Across the nighttime cyclorama shone as many stars as Craig had managed to pierce holes in the metal pie plates clamped to the lights.

Days and nights slipped into one another as electricity was released—or throttled to a comforting hum in the transformers. One long night we passed on the terrace of a penthouse upon cushioned wrought-iron porch furniture beside paper geraniums in papier-mâché planters. The horizon gleamed with the spires of skyscrapers Craig had stamped into a template that afternoon. The moon was a huge and incandescent old-fashioned limelight perched just behind the cheaters; the block of burning lime kept twisting and rising into the jet of ignited gas—dangerous, all terribly dangerous, I'm sure, but which full moon is not?

Restless that night, I got up and went wandering backstage, down into the open dressing rooms. Beside a union notice on the bulletin board is a telegram congratulating "Fred" on an opening now ancient. A border of small bulbs outlines the communal mirror in which I can make out my own dim face but can imagine a host of brilliant fools, at once impudent and sober, staring into their gleaming reflections—Tartaglia, Scapino, Trivelino, Mescolino, Scatolino, Colafronio, Pulcinella, Burattino, Gradelino—above the still-seated Argentina, Rosetta, Columbina and Pasquella, who presses red satin circles to her cheeks, then grinds out her cigarette in a shallow, silvered disc of an ashtray. Only the ghost of a handprint, rapidly fading, distinguishes the mirror from the room. I run a finger over a leather mask on the table: bulbous nose, a wart as big if not as cool as a robin's egg, an open mouth in the horsehair beard. A box by the door sprouts ten wooden swords and a pair of stilts, one pushed deeper down than the other, their braced footrests the tentative steps toward heaven in an ascent forgotten, or in any case abandoned.

Down a long, low-ceilinged corridor I make my way, accompanied overhead by pipes hot with com-

pressed steam that hisses, condenses and drips to
the concrete floor from a loose fitting. A metal door
lined with asbestos trolleys opens at my touch, a
cylindrical sandbag hung from a greased pulley
wire doing the work. In the storage room beyond
are racks of painted flats. I can see only their bor-
ders: a Doric column against a stormy sky; the
corner window of an all-night diner framing a seated customer in a trilby, his back to me but his face
turned to address whom I'll never know; maroon
wallpaper cut off by a cream chair rail highlighted
and shadowed to appear thrown in relief; the tan
brush of a lion's tail suspended in mid-flick against
the distant, murderous leaves of a yucca. The whole
theater, save for the rush of steam that suddenly
rattles the loose joint in the hallway, is silent and I
fancy myself the midnight prowler until I stand on
tiptoe, lift a shade and see a pair of nyloned legs
scissoring through a cold, wet, metropolitan afternoon.

I didn't like that glimpsed reminder of people in
shabby street clothes victimized by weather and
time, the world of errands done on lunch breaks—
and I fled back to the penthouse, the starry cyclorama and Craig. It was night. It was summer. We
were lovers. It was night. It was summer.

Craig had a beautiful indifference to human at-
tachments, longings, jealousies, all of which he considered "sticky." To him it was enough to exercise,
eat well, build sets and plot lights. If I told him I
was becoming fond of him he would go vague and
polite, as an atheist does when forced to bow his

head for grace at the annual family dinner. He must have sensed that my feelings were beams trained on you that had spilled over onto him, and he asked me to talk about you.

I did so reluctantly. This hesitation wasn't prompted by reticence—as you know, I'll tell anyone anything. But (surely you understand) I had tried so long and with so little success to forget you. Craig's contempt for love, or rather his dismissal of it, had struck me as modern and sensible, and I had yearned to imitate him. He would teach me; I'd be his scholar. And now, here I was, beginning our story again, an old role I knew too well and had played too long if not lately. The lines came back to me, one by one, their intonations guided by the familiar verse, the gestures and smiles perfectly timed, automatic in the delivery but once expressed recalling the emotions they will always signify.

Craig and I were sitting on a bearskin rug (dyed nutria over a thickening layer of sponge rubber) before a fire (the reflections cast by a rotating drum of crinkled aluminum foil spotlit with amber and red). Although he was intelligent so long as he was in flight, hovering around a thought, tugging at it, poking, wrestling it free, snapping it up, the moment he had to sit still to listen he began to frown and his lips parted as if, when he was grounded, he lost his talent to understand. His face was a charming compromise between the graceful girl and the hairy, aggressive boy within him, but when he tried to attend to what I was telling him the compromise broke down into its warring opposites. The girl, too timid to concentrate, gained control over his eyes, cloudless blue heavens darkened by twin lunar-eclipsed suns. And the girl also ruled his forehead, thin, taut silk worried by wind ripples—a girl one could picture being led by her parents up the staircase to the swelling din of her first dance, a moody, fragile girl lifted out of her daydreams and instructed to say clever things to adults and to expose her shoulders to tall men; or a rich, protected girl glancing for the first time into a dark shack teeming with children and hungry animals—a girl, that is, being reluctantly and without preparation initiated into an active, alien world.

But the boy had his own surlier response when his angry eyebrows, black grease marks joined above the nose by a passage of gold stippling, lowered into threatening horizons above those tremulous skies or when his shaved but heavily bearded upper lip twisted into a snarl and exposed a wet canine. Then he chewed on something and, save for the frightened eyes, the entire face, bristling with male force, exposed its elaborate rigging, as though the pale skin were a topsail turned transparent. And indeed his body, tormented by my demands, seemed to strain away from me, to run before the wind I had become, the gust of my desire—oh, he was a trim ship. His high instep was a ballerina's but the hairy legs not a boy's but a man's, and the slender, smooth waist feminine but the low voice masculine, and if I compare him to a bird or a ship I do so only because he is that elegant, that fleet, and that avid of flight.

"I'm sorry," he murmured, when I interrupted myself to ask if I was annoying him. "But I don't understand you. Perhaps—" and he moved up to the footlights, which silhouetted his slim body with purple gloom and his rising, open hand—"perhaps if we staged it. Put it on somehow. Then I could see it." Now *I* could see his features again; he'd returned to my side and the revolving cylinder simulating flames.

The theater gave a performance and on that evening I hid up on a catwalk and shivered, a water-damaged velveteen robe of royal blue clothing my nakedness. The lobby and auditorium doors had been thrown open an hour before curtain to chill the house, which the crowd would all too soon re-heat. A twine-bound box of programs, hurled out of a truck, was dragged up the steps by the head usher, opened, sorted.

Deep in the underground vaults below the stage, actors are beginning to make their entrances—here's a cheery hello from the *jeune premier*. He's greeting the wardrobe mistress, who tonight appears to be in truth a woman kept by a trunk, so motley is she in frayed slippers, a dirty cardigan sporting twenty straight pins for last-minute fittings, patched culottes and a brooch that may be her personal adornment but more probably is a make-do badge of office for the walk-on in Act Three.

Members of the chorus dribble, then pour in, their voices too loud and too clear, too trained. Though they arrive alone—brave, casual figures, hands deep in trench coats, a flight bag slung over one shoulder—they quickly burst into conversations about sore feet or sore throats, new union rules, upcoming auditions, one entertainer's overdose and another's obsession with a Sicilian twelve-year-old purchased for a song from the child's obliging mother. As they natter their hands dip into shoe boxes and rise hairy with caterpillars that cling to their faces as eyebrows or moustaches. A white line drawn down the bridge lends character to an anonymous nose; mascara supplies a dark flutter to a blond's lashes; lips and cheeks, pallid in the dressing-table glare, pick up color from carmined fingertips. Half-hour, and now the talk turns to the theater critic, so drunk the other night that he slept through two acts though unconsciousness did not keep him from panning Mary as Meg. Tonight's villain remarks that the critic is not the English lord he makes out to be but a Cockney—"And the *h* keeps falling off his typewriter just to spite him."

Ten minutes is called and five dancers, not on till the third act ballet, are already stretching at the barre in bulky gray sweatsuits, while a sixth shows a seventh the new combination put in yesterday: plié, changement, then this, then an attitude en pointe held for three beats, Nancy's entrance, and we're off downstage right. The curtain lowers with an electric hiss; through the fabric I can hear a solitary conscientious clarinetist practicing again and again a bass trill ending in a run up through the chalumeau. A gaffer crawls up beside me and adjusts a fresnel; I withdraw into a dark, precarious corner.

Now a trumpet essays a flourish, a second violin embarks on a dull continuo passage, the harpist strums a glissando, resets two of her seven pedals and strums again, the sixth and seventh dancers emerge from behind a wagon in the wings that is freighted with a gazebo trellised in plastic vines, wriggle their toes in a rosin box and go through the new steps on stage this time. While they're on point two stagehands carry a flat between their erect, trembling figures and deposit it behind a tormentor. The stage manager at his desk runs through the prompt-book, hesitates over one cue and has a whispered consultation on the intercom with the fellow on the follow-spot. The prompter in jeans smokes a cigarette with the conductor in tails. All the instruments are warming up, and I wonder what melodic pattern will be machine-stitched out of this ragbag of bleeps, drum rolls, pizzicatti and muted hoots. "Places, places," the manager calls and the dancers scamper off as the chorus, coroneted or cowled, gather like the great dead in the subdued margin of history.

From my vantage I can see the stars below, now arrayed in a constellation of seven women, though one of the Pleiades is so small she is lost behind the heaving and glistening body of another, now extinguished to a sole giant in black velvet whose ringed hand jerks up toward me as he plucks a stone harp, and now shining as two innocent virgins in the midst of white-robed nuns holding tapers that tremble before their hymn to happiness and love; curtain, interlude, panicked dollying and flying away of one set as another creaks on and the lights dim to a nocturnal blue. Whispering sailors mourn the death of a visibly breathing hero on the raked, rocking deck of a caravel outfitted with square-rigged sails ghostly against a midnight-dark cyclorama as dry ice smoke pours from blowers held in hands just behind sight lines. The soprano in a blonde wig and muslin robe laments something from the fo'c'sle, accompanied only by a guitar and a tambourine; pirates board the vessel and the curtain descends on swordplay and a vigorous tutti. I fell asleep on my perch, like a caged parrot on a high strut dreaming of the rumorous, steamy jungle. When my outstretched green wings had carried me up the river to the thundering falls, I awakened to the final bows of a cast in coronation clothes. A snooze later and they were gone, the gazebo remained unexplained, the house was silent, a work light glimmered from a black cord below me, and Craig, nude and warm, was holding my face between his hands, kissing me as seriously as though he were a father and I the child whose fever had finally broken.

The theater bore no traces of the departed invaders save for the smell of crushed-out cigarettes and snow-soaked fur coats and the sight of discarded programs littering the floor like the paillettes ripped off the dress of a woman fleeing the ball. Craig had worked on the production as a technician and I found charming the indentations of weariness impressed on a face whose youth seldom betrayed exertion or even emotion. From his tenderness I could tell he was worried about how I had fared. His solicitude gratified me at the same moment it made me wary. We love to give help but only to those who have no need of it, or more properly to those who desperately need it but proudly or despairingly refuse to accept it. We reach toward unreachable men in distress and toward no others. Self-sufficiency may inspire admiration but not love; frank, hungry need excites pity but tranquilizes desire. Why this should be so I have no idea, but I knew my eager distress simultaneously rendered me more sympathetic to Craig and less attractive. Experience has taught me (I'm not bitter, really I'm not) something about these hydraulics of passion.

"Where would you like to sleep tonight?" Craig asks me. And I, not wanting to confess anywhere will do so long as I'm in his arms, murmur, "On the moon." We empty the stage and he covers it with two piles of fiberglass rocks and a muslin dropcloth that flows down into a crater (a platform lowered a foot below the floor); on the cyclorama he projects a large, crisp earth. Beside our crater he plants the national flag and into the hole we crawl, naked, freezing, gasping for oxygen and so light that, were there air, a wind could whirl us away. The cast image of the earth becomes your familiar face, rounder and more marked with age than I had remembered it, watching me even now that I'm way beyond your gravitational pull.

Somehow I've failed to work out and Craig, a little disappointed in me, invites Thomas to live with us. Once before I'd seen Thomas at a party, unshaved and speechless, brooding in a winged armchair but thrusting cleated, orange boots out into the room. The boots were caked with mud too raw to be from this part of the country; his waist was circled by a belt made of silver medallions laced together which, if the observer squinted, fused into

74

a luminous, turning ring; in the depths of his chair his face was pale and long, the already high cheekbones raised higher by the cross-hatched steel engraving of his beard. The silvered waist was the zone I preferred and described to myself as "aristocratic," coming as it did between the feudal splendors of his face and the modern brutishness of his boots. But his face, despite my determination to prefer his waist, kept drawing me back. One eye was blue, the other green, the magical result of a child's chemistry experiment. Beside the green eye was drawn a curious birthmark on his temple, which I saw variously as the lair of those blushes that so often raided his cheeks or as the stinging imprint of the first hand that had slapped into breathing an infant who, though now a man, still resented delivery.

The situation at the theater quickly stabilized into a familiar and excruciating structure. Far from being the defiant and distant young man he appeared to be, Thomas had the capacity and desire to consign himself completely to us. We were the big brothers, or perhaps the parents, he'd always longed to interest, and now our interest in him was compulsive. Craig was held by Thomas's beauty and innocence; Thomas received the attention in confused but grateful silence; Craig prized and matched his silence, as though it were an original mode Thomas had invented rather than the simple, inadvertent expression of awkwardness I judged it to be; the vault of ice congealing around the lovers begged to be broken, and I did the chipping. Just as open scissors suggest snipping, an idle knife stabbing, coffee scalding, so their faces, inclined toward one another but not touching, called for the closure of the kiss, even if I had to arrange it, even if by arranging it I ensured my own suffering.

Now I loved Craig and he loved Thomas and Thomas loved Craig, but both these men could communicate only through me, as though one were the airwaves striking the eardrum and the other the fluid vibrating across the triggered hairs of the basilar membrane; for air to touch liquid it had to pass through the anvil, stirrup and hammer, and I served the function of those delicate bones.

To console me, Craig would draw me aside and assure me that Thomas was no more than an infatuation, a delightful boy from the provinces, an indoor amusement during the cold spell. And wasn't it funny the way Thomas could not finish a sentence without sinking into a mumbled "And whatever and whatever"? And had I noticed the way Thomas, embarrassed by a tarnished molar, pursed his lips unnaturally when he laughed? I had not.

The other misguided tactic Craig adopted to assure me how trivial his attachment to Thomas must be was his repeated insistence that their only bond was sexual. That their ardor might be all the more intense, Craig dressed us in wing-tipped collars and cutaways and placed us in a Victorian sitting room, me in a horsehair-stuffed rocker and them on an ottoman. A grandfather clock ticked (or rather a tape just behind the flocked flat looped around and around past a magnetic head, feeding its solemn knocking into the house speakers). A gas lamp glowed on the table beside me, its penumbra boosted by an overhead spotlight. From a distance the antimacassars under my elbows might have appeared to be lace, but up close they were clearly plastic sprayed to dull their sheen. I wore age makeup, but their faces were cosmetically young. We spoke in unnaturally loud voices in order to project to the top balcony of the empty house. Behind the frosted windows (glass sponged with Epsom salts and beer) the cyclorama darkened from sunset pinks and flamingos into the massing blues of dusk. I kept pouring an empty teapot into empty cups as we made witty small talk with such fastidious diction that the explosive *p*'s, *t*'s and *d*'s sent sheets of spray flying from our mouths into the cross-lit, shadowless room. After this (presumably humorous) spate of polite chatter my guests stretched conspicuously and feigned yawns and begged to retire. I led them downstage left along a path designated by tape on the floor to a bedroom that Thomas surreptitiously tugged in from the wings by pulling a thin lead of fishing tackle that had been left lying on the floor. When I asked the young men if they thought the quilt would provide sufficient warmth on such a bitterly cold night, Craig comically tugged at his collar to indicate embarrassment and Thomas, equally uncomfortable, stifled a cough in his hand. Blushes flew down from their haven, the birthmark. Once the door (flimsy plywood stained and grained to resemble massive oak) is closed into its unsteady frame, the guests collapse into each other's arms, groan with pleasure, draw apart to place a warning finger to their lips, undress with ecstatic haste, dive into the four-poster and draw its curtains shut. Just before they vanish from sight into this sea of ruffles, the high-spirited lads pop their heads out of the surf, one head above the other, and wink at the nonexistent audience.

Back in the parlor I seek distractions, first lifting a book, then discarding it in favor of a stereoscopic viewer, finally tiptoeing back to the bedroom door, to which I apply a guilty, greedy ear. Up to this point the scene is staged as farce and timing, miming, vocal tricks, double takes and innuendoes are played strictly for laughs. But now the style of the piece shifts. The character I'm representing dons a child's sailor suit and sits in the hallway outside the closed bedroom door and cries. He talks to himself. A smile flickers across his lips, only to vanish when the eyes go big and dead and the jaw drops into a sob. After starting on a high whine, the sob rumbles into the bass register and breaks off into a succession of muted yelps. The body lengthens on the floor, face down, then rolls to one side as the knees contract toward the chest.

"Okay, okay, that's enough for today," Craig says, helping me up. He has changed into jeans though he's still shirtless. A light just behind Thomas's head prevents me from reading his expression, but I can see he's pushed back the bed curtains and pulled the sheet up to his shoulders. He's smiling, the cigarette held in a tapering hand rendered longer and lighter by its subtle tremor. Craig, supporting me, leads me to a dressing room where he makes me tea with an electric coil in a mug. Much later,

returning with Craig to the stage, I observe that
Thomas has changed the scenery before leaving. In
place of the Victorian sitting room is a misty forest,
layer after layer of foliage sewn to half-lowered
scrims, one dropped behind the other. The many
lights are gelled blue or green and all held down to
only a few points of illumination. Paper flowers are
strewn across the floor and the ogival shadows of
leaves play across our moving hands; the sound of
our footsteps through underbrush is simulated
offstage by Thomas trampling a burlap bag filled
with flake glue. As we approach an old tree, thick
as a giant's waist, the trunk opens to admit us to a
secret bower canopied with luscious woodbine,
sweet musk roses and eglantine. Craig places an
animal's head over my own and sheds his clothes
until he is as smooth and pale as melting candlewax
at the moment it brims over its oily cup and slides
down the firm taper. And indeed, in just this way,
he seems to grow, burn, offer warmth and pliancy
but promise, if the moment's missed, to be cold and
rigid. He bends toward me and opens his mouth to
kiss the snout of my mask. He gazes into my, or
rather the animal's, eyes, though mine are just behind the empty holes he adores. He whispers
phrases loving and passionate and they are just the
words I've longed to hear but cannot, muffled as
my ears are by the thickness of the costume skull.
Now he rises, stands over me, and if I lift or lower
my head I can scan the length of his lean body
through the peepholes of my papier-mâché mask.
Should I bray my praise? Lights within our bower
have dawned to make him clearer, brighter, and he

is still speaking. I can't decide which I want more—
to hear him or to look at him, to enjoy my blissful
torment or to gauge by his endearments my chances
at future bliss . . . or torment. I feel that he must return, at least to some small extent, a devotion that
has become my entirety.

Though I am confined in a trumpery mask and
he has donned cellophane wings stretched over
veins of wire, and a diligent and not very bright but
repentant and frightened Thomas is running the
lights, awaiting his next cue, Craig fans my bestial
cheek with painted butterflies and offers a bunch of
plastic grapes, outsize for visibility, to my black
leather lips. Although my real mouth is compressed
with chagrin and the lust of a true lover—which is
metasexual, since it longs to possess the sternum,
femur, cranium and the muscles and skin that bind
one bone to another only if that union will further
his chances of owning the *soul*—although my real
mouth is a hard line of pain, I oblige him by nuz-
zling the fruit and batting the beast's huge lashes
(I've found the exact angle at which the weighted
lids close). Much as I resent the mask, the crepe
flowers, the hot lights, and the small overhead
branches faked out of twine, sized, wound in cloth,
painted and stiffened with wire, I recognize that no
lover ever presented himself with any fewer impediments, and that this setting at least has the merit of
proclaiming the inevitable sense of unworthiness
and artificiality.

But now Craig has become inspired and he rises
ever higher above the animal at his feet; he paces
around me with the tact and forbearance of a god

who knows that by answering a mortal's prayer and appearing before him, the gift may blind the devotee or strike him dumb and will certainly unsuit him to the rest of his ordinary days. Yet the daring god believes that the visit must at least be memorable. If it is to bring so much loss, it should be worth losing and therefore, as the air above the altar takes on flesh, as the neck emerges out of the smoke, white wisps curling into the curve of these precise shoulders, blue haze concentrating into blue eyes, gray scarf of burned incense layering thicker and thicker into the lifting, outstretched, beckoning hand, the god cautiously steals up on his supplicant, at first a visual trick, no more than the result of the late hour, the secret ritual, the prolonged fast, the very need for some sign, an illusion to be blinked away, only later a palpable suggestion, finally an undeniable reality. He speaks to me; I cannot understand him (why did I assume I would know a god's language?). He is immense and pale as ash blown off the cold blackened log, fierce with his own strength that he prefers to veil . . . to spare me. And at every moment my mind flickers back and forth between thinking no, he is a representation, surprisingly tangible, of a power that can never be seen and yes, he is in fact here, seen and seeing. To lay to rest my doubts about his literal appearance in my room, he touches me, pushes me down, makes love to me, but too slowly, with too much control to satisfy my need. It is an act that we are engaged in, and I do not have the reserve or the fortitude to proceed, step by delicious and aching step, through an act. I stiffen at the wrong moment, gaze up into his healthy face with despair at the impersonality of his desire (no matter that the desire is for me) and the only consolation I can formulate is the thought that, since he is a god, he already knows and has forgiven my panic. The weighted lids tip shut. I need not be a good lover; he is an echo to his own shout.

When I awaken, bruised and humiliated, last night's costume disgusts me. I kick the empty head away and sidle, disgruntledly and nursing a sore right shoulder, down a corridor toward the green room. There I walk in on Craig and Thomas, both of them sprawling in canvas chairs, chewing gum and looking unpleasantly smug and idle. As Thomas listens, Craig rambles on about his own amazing muscular coordination and acute kinesthetic sensitivity, a discourse I've heard before in which he will refer with awe to Energy. Thomas is prepared to speak to me and does wink with the green eye and wave feebly in my direction (though with a cowardly hand hidden from Craig by the back of the chair) but he's taking his cues from his companion, who has apparently decided that to ask me how I slept or even to greet me would be an admission of guilt. From his loud, cheerful voice I deduce that any complaint I might make would draw from him a studied, overly polite expression of incomprehension. "Please begin again at the beginning. Now, you're *offended* about last night? Yes? You are? But *why?*" Morosely I plunge the electric coil into a dirty cup.

I knew I had to leave the theater, but before I

did there was one more thing I wanted to explore.

I drew Craig aside and said I'd be going away in a few hours. He swallowed his gum, took my hand and lost his slouching, leg-swinging insolence. He attempted to dissuade me from leaving; he apologized for everything; then he agreed to help me. I told him that when we lived together you had loved me with the impious desire I had felt for the first time only last night, felt within the bole of the giant tree—a desire that I had felt for him, Craig. Of course, as I made clear, I must have loved you all along, even from the beginning, but for me the sentiment had been careless, lazy, devoid of passion, the infant's hand, translucent fingers and meaty palm, stretching into the milk-rich, meshed twilight, confident of touching the mouth of its adoring mother. We are born with only one fear, the fear of falling, and that primeval anxiety now held me as I plummeted farther and farther away from your indifferent hands, which are tucked under your arms, visible (since you've turned your back) only as slightly protruding fingertips, polyps pulsing in sluggish water. No chance of stopping my fall, of being hovered back up to you by a squadron of pink and gold cherub heads outfitted with wings but not with bodies. Falling, scintillating, a diminishing star shifting, as I recede ever further, into the red band of the visible spectrum, I can only rehearse my time with you, the blue, hazy days spied through gauze curtains exhaled and slowly, thoughtfully inhaled by the open windows. You loved me as I loved Craig—with this difference, that your face was masked only by glasses always slightly askew, one pane smudged with a thumbprint and both dusty, and your love endured for years, silent and patient.

"I want to live through those days again," I tell Craig, "but with me playing his role and you mine. You look as I did then—small, blond, too young for your eighteen years."

The first moment we re-created was that time you watched me sleep. You had first met me in Spain the year before and brought me home. Initially I had been so bewildered by your love, your friends, your celebrity that I had submitted to everything patiently and gratefully. But then I had decided I had to amount to something on my own, go to college, live by myself. That experiment ended in disaster, of course, but for one year I was a diligent student. I wouldn't make love to you—that was bad, that was a distraction, that meant I still belonged to you, not to myself. I held down two jobs, attended classes, studied, made my meals, studied some more.

Hastily Craig and I assembled that dingy student apartment as best I could recollect it and we could approximate it from among our props and flats. In one room on a narrow cot covered with an army blanket Craig lay dozing fully dressed in the button-down shirt and ironed chinos of that era. He was exhausted from the two jobs, the studies. There were ink stains on the index finger of his right hand.

I entered silently, sat beside the sleeping boy for a moment, then wandered about the other room. A study lamp on an extension arm shed the cold blue glow of lonely concentration on an open Latin book turned to a list of irregular verbs. And here is the open wardrobe, the few clothes—the other pair of chinos, two shirts on hangers, the thin winter coat. And there is the kitchen stocked with staples and lentils, the nutritious meat "substitute." Oh, my friend, so you saw me, and you later told me that you realized only then, that night when you let yourself into my apartment, that I was leading a life of my own, that I had my own ambitions, my self-imposed discipline, my integrity. You had loved me so intensely that you'd convinced yourself you had invented me. That moment while I dozed convinced you that it was not my sole purpose to torture you, that I had not moved out and refused your money to spite you. You saw that I had other interests. Latin, for instance. Ironing my chinos. Baking a lentil loaf.

Beside my bed, on the floor, was a looking glass. As I slept you lit a candle and held the mirror up and studied my reflection. Now I did so, watching the flame brighten and draw Craig's childlike face out of the shadows, then dim and float him back into darkness, just as the sun during a polar winter rises only to set.

The following summer I continued to take courses until I was so nervous and exhausted I became ill and you took me back in. For you that summer was our sweetest season together (I can scarcely recall it, forgive me). During those hot days I was always dressed in baggy white shorts and a T-shirt, I think, and I was always racing to work or school on my English bicycle (the only gift from you I'd kept). You and I slept together almost every night but I, confused and frightened by your ardor and exhausted by work and classes, had taken a vow of chastity. For me it was little more than a joke, but you took the vow terribly seriously. You were content not to make love to me so long as no one else did. We had a *mariage blanc* and you explained what that meant.

Because there was no sexual release, everything became erotic for you. Even the sound of my approaching bicycle. Or so you've said. You'd be walking along (as I was now past a backdrop of buildings) and in the airless heat of that deserted summer street you'd hear the sound of my revolving rear wheel tick-tick-ticking, slipping over the stationary gears as I coasted to a halt, one foot standing on a pedal. A block away the whirr was so faint you'd sometimes turn, a welcoming smile on your lips and greet—the empty street; you'd mistaken for my approach the accelerating wheel of your own circling thoughts spinning around the fixed idea of you, me, you, me, you and me, unity . . . .

To me it was nothing, nothing at all. That bike I junked ages ago. That summer I was worried about my weight, which I had to fight to maintain by consuming whole loaves of bread, slice by gagging slice, each heavy with honey. And I hated my schedule; I was probably feeling sorry for myself. You pleased me with compliments I didn't trust and startled me with inexplicable bursts of affection. Now, as I try to understand you by impersonating you, as I seize Craig's hand and press a kiss to his dirty palm, I am more struck by his accurate portrayal of my old embarrassment than with any new understanding of why you made that demonstration there, in the middle of the street at noon. You said, "See, they've emptied the city just for us. It's ours. Everyone's gone away out of politeness," and I say those words to Craig, but he retrieves his hand and uses it to hoist the bicycle to his shoulder (time for an afternoon session with the bread). His precision in recapturing my exact response is uncanny; I haven't prompted him. If your odd kiss and whimsical words can *still* evoke the same reaction, then can I be blamed for what I did? Could I have behaved otherwise? I had to hold you off.

And the recognition that I never had a choice, yet have had to suffer the consequences of a decision I supposedly made, angers me. I've searched for you and not found you, attempted to forget you and found you everywhere, in foreign children, in my own childhood memories, in the bodies of hundreds of men I've ransacked, tearing them open as though surely this one must be concealing the contraband goods, only to throw them aside, meaningless raffia, and I've watched my own face age as I waited for your return, fearing I would no longer attract you should I ever see you again . . .

"Stop," I say to Craig. "Let's not go on." He comes back down the stairs with the bicycle and sets it on the ground, propping its weight on the kickstand, searching my face for an explanation. The curtain, lowered till now, rises swiftly and in the dark auditorium I fancy you're sitting, watching me. You're pitiless. You think that now at last the play is beginning.

CHAPTER VI

After my mother's death I was enrolled in a boarding school and I seldom heard from my father—a Christmas greeting or a postcard from Morocco of a water-seller, gilt cups and velvet clothes, something mailed three months before I received it. The bills and my meager spending money were handled by a lawyer, as was an absurdly large clothes allowance, half of which was mailed directly to a local haberdasher, the remainder to a downtown tailor. These arrangements turned me into a penniless dandy. The trousers Giuseppe made for me were pocketless (the reigning fashion, as far as I could deduce from slick magazines, though no other living man I knew seemed to follow it). The other boys laughed at my cashmeres, tweeds, vests, gartered stockings, silk foulards, the houndstooth stalking cap and the velvety brown fedora (no matter how I crushed it, the fedora, like a starlet in a horror film, assumed a beguiling pose), but I wore these costumes with a mixture of chagrin and pride—they were pledges that would someday be redeemed, the accoutrements of a glamorous life I was about to lead with my father.

My school had been built on the estate of a whimsical tycoon whose taste ran to artificial lakes stocked with fat, whiskered goldfish resembling Tartar khans; he also delighted in brand-new temples constructed in ruins, the columns installed fallen, the features of statues preweathered. The Scottish gardeners outnumbered the masters; the dining hall was vaster and more gothic than Chartres. My house master, the exasperated martinet, conducted white-glove inspections of our monastically plain cells every morning at seven. At night, during the "free" half-hour before lights out, he lingered around the open stall toilets, his ginger whiskers wet with drops of whiskey. Later he would summon his favorite of the moment to his apartment and measure the boy's shivering body with a tape by way of determining his development and prospects for joining the soccer team next quarter. I was never invited, though I made many unnecessary and forbidden trips to the fountain, my bare feet tiptoeing through the band of charged light escaping through the space at the bottom of the housemaster's locked door.

In no way did I distinguish myself. Too small to play sports, too abstracted to shine in class, too fearful to make friends, I glided from dorm to chapel to classroom to the stuffy, echoing study hall as noiselessly as a cloud in trousers. I never cheated. I never won a prize or placed in a competition. I had no relatives and, during holidays, I had no place to go.

But, as best as I can recall, those days were far from bleak. The concentration I was able to apply to even the least conspicuous object (the diagonal scratch in the bottom left window pane in my room) filled my routine with menace, the subtle allusion to other windows I had seen smashed or painted black. In the first frost glinted bits of diamond; I recalled the hammer on the back stairs. The barber came at me with his clippers—Jasper's raw neck. When I strode through hundreds of daffodils down a hill I had named Rumor (since I regarded the flowers as wagging tongues), an unsuspecting collie crossed my path. We label the feelings of our childhood with the names we learn as adults and brightly, confidently, refer to that old "anguish" or "despair" or "elation." The confidence of liars. For those words meant nothing to us then; what we lacked as children was precisely the power to designate and dismiss, and when we describe the emotions of one age with the language of another, we are merely applying stickers to locked trunks, calling "fragile" or "perishable" contents that, even were we to view them again, would be unrecognizable. But come, let us jimmy the hasp and lift the lid.

The morning bell is ringing, summoning me to breakfast. My bed is rich with the warmth and odor of my own body, soup cauldron on the simmer. I ladle myself up out of those depths and look across the cold black courtyard at other boys' rooms, illuminated one by one to reveal, on the first floor, bare feet touching bare wood, and on the second a pimply face gazing into his own still disappointing reflection. As I pull at clothes in the closet my hands enjoy the cold wools and the colder silks lining jackets, though I'm saddened momentarily by the hollow yelp of a hanger sliding across the metal bar. The shrilling of bells down corridors polished by rotary brushes into spirals as individual as thumbprints; the thunder of scuffed shoes pounding and falling down carpetless stairs and then— once outside in the courtyard, which is silent under the stars—transformed into a dry, crisp clatter; the teasing delirium of voices and the clanking of spoons against cereal bowls, a noise hopelessly insignificant within the groined vastness of that hall, filling in now as pink light exorcises gray stone ghosts—did I *find* those winter dawns sad or do their echoes sadden me only now? Just as the haughty stars that dwarfed and mocked us had long since died, so that eager but hushed throng of boys (the crewcut wrestler with the courtly manner and cynical tongue, the science zombie who wept over sentimental records, the fatty fascist who lost weight and turned communist, lost his heart and became an esthete)—these boys wrestle, weep and strike attitudes only in my memory, however dimly they move behind the rattling panes our breath steamed white.

By the time we assembled for chapel heaven had vanished, the stars screened from view by blue sky. Our spires and battlements had burned their way clear of mist, our murmurs and footfalls had become loud enough to fill up whole rooms, and the wood organ pulsed bright and dim in cloudswept sunlight. The singing stops and the handsome, facetious face of our chaplain appears above a clerical collar he has turned into a joke, as though his vestments were no less absurd than the sacred texts he reads with raised eyebrows and a suppressed chuckle or the hymns we bawl out: "By the light of burning martyrs, we tread the bloody trail."

Snow dashed over flagstones, raced up a turret or crumbled under its own weight off a wall, cracking, sagging—and then, caught in a blast of wind, blew sky-high into flickering gestures. As these white heroics—pursuits, escapes, blinding bombardments—besieged the courtyard, the chaplain placidly made the day's announcements. Another bell, and we all hurried off to examine the new "unsat" list, which named the dunces whose grades were unsatisfactory and would be taken off the playing fields and returned to the afternoon study hall.

Neither unsat nor securely seated, and certainly not athletic, I was a curious specimen: a student with his afternoons off. Had the masters ever focused on my status it would have been changed. Knowing my freedom depended upon remaining inconspicuous, I kept myself camouflaged, timing my movements with the shadows of clouds, placing my tweed jacket against the stubble of dead grass, concealing my shock of blond hair in a dart of sunlight glancing off a distant window pane. Once I was safe in my room I bolted the door, which was forbidden, and brewed coffee on a hot plate, doubly forbidden. Then I played a record of a chanteuse so softly that she sounded like the samba singer in the tub drain who comes to taunt the man home from his holiday. Outside the courtyard was as lifeless as Rio on Ash Wednesday.

From the same magazine that pictured my exotic clothes I learned that my father had attended an October in Madrid ball (held in London), had been "seen" with Zizi de la Felucca (a former Miss America), drank Sidecars before breakfast, would be hunting in Ireland, escorted some dictator's widow somewhere—and hoped to bring spats back. Since I never bothered to date my clippings and all those places (Estoril, Alexandria, Cap Ferrat) were at best vague imaginings to me, the various social events soon merged and my father became ubiquitous, less a man in time than a synchronous field of energy. When one boy laughed at a dawn-blue tie mailed to me from Charvet's, I told him, "But I'm not dressing for you. I belong to another world," exactly as though I were comparable to Samsaki Charuchinda, the exchange student recently arrived from Bangkok (already "Sam" to some) who came trailing saffron clouds, having just been released from a six-month stint at a Buddhist monastery, where he learned little of the Way but several ways to tell fortunes and cast spells. Among his titles was one that could be translated "Prince."

The letter summoning me wasn't written by my father, of course, but by the woman he lived with that summer. "Last night we were having supper with some new friends outside on a terrace, an indecently late Spanish meal that wasn't half-bad and that ended in Baked Alaska, of all things, which the Spanish for some reason think of as 'English' (does it resemble their *zuppa inglese*—or is that Italian?), when our hosts' son showed up, one of those lads in short pants who's still a child only because the Spanish haven't invented adolescence yet, I guess, and he was lots of fun, very jolly, and it was droll

93

hearing his English (though everyone soon reverted
to French to my horror, since I can't understand a
word of French though I speak it fluently—is it the
way the words run together, the *liaison*, which makes
me think of sauce thickening or politics, no help to
me, I can assure you) and later, back at our villa,
your pop said he had a 'brat' (don't be insulted, all
in good fun, you know) with much more 'class' than
that boy. Fierce paternal pride! He produced a
snapshot of you, hopelessly mutilated and out-of-
date, even so I could see you were a delight, so we
thought it would be fun for you to join us, almost
instantly, specially since your father's obsessed with
bullfights these days and I'm allergic to the gore
and would love a playmate. I hope you're still fair.
I'm a blonde and young enough to be mistaken for
your sister, I trust."

The letter ended in enough X's to win two tit-
tat-toe games but no signature, no directions or
timetables, no money, nor any confirmation that the
plan had been approved by my father. Nevertheless
I wrote the lawyer who handled Dad's affairs in
America and said that my father insisted I sail to
Spain the day after school let out. Daddy wanted
him, the lawyer, to make all the arrangements. I
would also need traveling money.

Crossing an ocean presented me with a free week
to sort out my past and make decisions regarding
the future, and every day I would rise to that discreet knock on the cabin door. But first there was
the more pressing decision about whether to shave
today or wait until tomorrow, then the greater question as to whether I should sit with the Bryersons or

94

not, that retired admiral and his wife who had so playfully and suavely drawn me into saying a pack of lies that now was quickly multiplying into several decks—the A deck where my stateroom could be found, the B deck where we swam, and a whole nether world of decks below the water line, submerged kings and queens, a diving ace, the weeping sailor, the drowned joker and the royal flush spreading across my cheeks when the Bryersons questioned closely the story I'd rattled off on the first night about my mother's refusal to drive her new roadster because she insisted it "bruised her sables." That's Mom for you, I told them, sweating and grinning. The couple exchanged a worried glance.

Once we'd landed in Spain I plunged on by train to Dad's resort. I had only my phrase book to comfort me—that and the mountain valleys opening up below me like invitations to lead other lives. There. I could switch places with that glossy-haired boy in short pants and place *my* hand on the door leading into a shuttered interior, lines of light on the whitewashed ceiling and wall, one awakening a silver flute within the brass bedstead, while he could be me, plummeting toward a palm-lined coast and a father remembered only as a drawl, the smell of Scotch and the smooth facing of a dinner jacket lapel.

Our family name made sense to Spanish ears only when pronounced in a manner as definite and assured as it was impossible for me to reproduce. I wrote it out and showed it to one taxi driver after another. The first merely shook his head (could he read?). A second excitedly drew a map in the air but just as his right index finger struggled to the top of a hill and the blessed panorama it commanded, he shrugged and jammed his hands back in his pockets. My salvation was a polyglot German jeweler who warned me I'd be arriving before the household was fully awake and dressed (it was noon); he asked me to remind my father that his hat had come back from London, this time with the *correct* initials stamped in gold on the sweatband.

How hard it is to recall anything about my first trip through that town! I guess I was so excited that the excess of emotion turned every patch of stucco glimpsed at a distance into his villa's walls, every scintilla into the flash off his monocle, every whiff of sulphur (the prevailing smell) into the odor of the hot springs where he bathed and from which he would be emerging, bare flesh ruddy and brilliantined hair a runny spectrum, oil and water iridescing into color-charged drops. Again and again each corner concealed a palace, hastily revised as we drew nearer into something small, inert but noisy until, rounding the bend, I watched the illusion vanish altogether—but just behind the next curve in the steep road a new chimera unfolded its gorgeous wings to dry in the sun: my wing, Dad's . . . Even the monotonous prattling of unseen children I could ascribe to his bastards, for surely he'd not been idle nor unfruitful. But would I appeal to his critical eye as I stood behind his other children, my hands resting on their shoulders, our faces turned toward the mild sun and the black bat of the curtained view camera flapping toward us

and preparing to open its metal mouth at the instant of contact and drink away the guilt and love
that pulsed within us?

The driver stopped before a gate set into a low
wall, deposited my luggage on the gravel, took some
of the paper money I helplessly proffered and returned coins, got back behind the wheel and, just
before driving off, mimed the slow opening of the
gate (his brown hand hinging at the wrist), the
rapid ascent of my feet (two fingers climbing the
air), hysterical hugs and liberal gulps of champagne
(a thumb exploded up out of a closed fist and was
then jammed between his lips as he tilted his head
farther and farther back, adam's apple glugging).
He disappeared, laughing and still sucking his
thumb.

I stared at my first cactus and hypothesized my
first lizard. Above the repeated vamping of crickets
hung a silence as demanding as the spotlight on a
singer too drunk to perform. But I entered that
expectation bravely and called out, "Hi! Hello!
Anybody here? Anyone awake?"

At the end of the path a pale curtain luffed in
the breeze. Tiptoeing through the open french
window and drawing back the curtain I introduced
light and myself into a room clearly meant to stay
dark and childless. Things were turning: a record,
though the needle was resting in its cradle; and a
pedestal from a showroom that was a foot high but
supported nothing. Glasses of every size, filled or
drained, covered every available surface, even the
floor, as though put out to catch rain under a rid-
dled ceiling. Someone had tied pink yarn bows

around the necks of rubber alligators, one of which had been hanged from the mantelpiece. An ashtray overflowed with butts. In a low-ceilinged room off the kitchen I found a gloomy maid wiping dishes and depositing them on a counter gummy with party favors; she looked up and sighed.

Down a corridor strewn with sleeping people and discarded clothing and overturned bottles was an open door. I picked my way over the debris and looked in. There was a fat man, bearded and bald, his beard a confusion of black and white whiskers, asleep, one hand flung back, the other at his side, touching the blond head of a man or woman otherwise concealed in sheets. The fat man's blue eye suddenly cocks open. "Yes?" he asks on two notes through something viscous in his throat, which he hawks onto the floor. "*Ingles?*" he demands, this time his voice under control. The room, screened by silk-lined yellow curtains, glowed like the heart of an apricot, though it smelled of apple brandy and French cigarettes. An enema bag's khaki tubing described the symbol for infinity on the majolica tiles.

"Hello, Dad, it's me."

The yellowing streak in his beard fell from his lip to his chin like a tusk, old ivory, but what fascinated me were the swirls of black hair on his chest, fine aerial roots clinging to the massive, deeply scarred trunk. "Who?"

"Your son," I suggested, wondering if I, too, would someday be that hairy, wondering if he'd deny me.

His other eye opened. A meaty hand unconsciously pulled the sheet over the gold head at his side that had begun to emit tiny groans. He experimented with a few gestures—one that did deny me, another that indicated confusion. The third was an embrace. As he rose he decorously wrapped a towel around his waist.

I tightened in his arms, aware that we were two strangers locked in an embarrassing social predicament, but after a moment a huge blind infant within me began to squall (Love? isn't it Love who wears a handkerchief tied over his eyes? who stays a baby?). The stuffy room dimmed like a medical amphitheater full of attention and darkness and all that remained visible was the surgeon, struggling to deliver me of this big baby.

I cried in that throbbing room, soaking his shoulder with tears, saliva and snot. He didn't push me away. I was home, even if home was a blonde woman bare-breasted above the sheets, or the dour peasant woman standing in the dark hallway staring at us, or the gathering revelers waking, kneeling and peeking out from behind the peasant's black skirts.

When the sobs stopped and the baby had been born, my father shifted me to his side and pressed his outstretched hand into my shoulder. He presented me to his bed companion, then turned me to the faces in the hallway. "My son," he said, in a voice hoarse with emotion. "My son," he repeated, and the sun brightened on cue, repainting the interior in harsher hues, bleaching out the blonde's face with titanium white, lending the black figures in the hallway marginal browns, grays and ochres and flinging off the beveled edge of a looking glass on the wall a single vertical stripe of light that transected someone's green iris, planting fire in the emerald.

My father was an immoral man. He used people as means to an end, the end his own amusement or, failing that, his temporary relief from boredom. Idle and idly curious, he would press his pudgy finger up any hole that was warm and living. He would go on long, chummy strolls with Henry, an English boy who visited us from time to time. At night he assembled the "time-wasters," as he called his companions, for long dinners on the veranda, and during those hours he showered everyone with attentions, as Jove showers Danae with his humid lust. He paced up and down the flagstones beside the glittering slab of linen between flambeaux that reeked of kerosene and, snatching dishes from the butler, handed them to the diners himself, bowing and chuckling all the while, condescending to fuss over Helene's disappointing appetite ("Here, you've neglected the spinach *véronique*. Don't you want the little white grapes at least? Try one. Permit me") or urging a tone-deaf youth with aspirations toward operetta to favor us with a zarzuela ("You know the one: 'This is his letter, he lives and loves me, what will he say, let's see, oh God, why can't I read?' My all-time favorite, adore, I adore unlettered love")— and with that he chucks lovely Linda from Texas under the chin as though in reference to her own adorable illiteracy, though he knows she can read because he watches her every afternoon in her folding chair scanning the personals in the *Herald*

Tribune for coded news as to the whereabouts of her coven of witches driven out of Paris one morning after a particularly sloppy mass. Dad's insulting favors are scattered here and there until, not eating but eternally sipping, sipping, as though he were a sacred cow and the clinking ice were pewter bells tied to his neck, he charges through the crowd, turns tables on their sides, bellows rage, breaks china in a shop where nothing is sold but everything, everyone can be bought. In the sulfurous night air the little cries of fleeing guests nip at the plush hem of Satan's cape and on a distant hill a motorbike sputters up the road. The only other sounds are running feet on gravel and the ratcheting of crickets feeding a bucket down a well that, after it is drawn up, will overflow with another molten sun.

Two rented cars await our party at the foot of the stairs. Until we see them we have no idea why my father has awakened us at nine and hurried us through breakfast. Now, with all of us assembled around him, he tells us that today we're off to Granada. Linda, holding her straw hat to her head with a fragile arm lifted up out of an organdy sleeve, tilts her lips—her most enthusiastic response. Usually she remains expressionless, handing her face to us reverently, as a jeweler places his best gem before a client. The maids, obviously pleased to see us going, pack the luncheon in the trunk.

"When," someone asks once we're underway, "when was the Alhambra built?" My father undertakes to explain. He mentions the Moors, makes Othello their leader, he has Desdemona (whose name, with its double *d*, elicits his stammer) beg for a cool, hilly retreat, a request that Othello lavishly fulfills. With a final burst of daring and authority, he answers, "It was all done in the tenth century." The time-wasters gaze at him in awe.

Only on occasion does he display his knowledge, as sparing with it as Linda is with her smiles. Yet his retinue has seen him more than once before an open book, usually an illustrated volume about Byzantium. He admires Byzantine political arrangements, as complex, static and theological as those in our own household. He has of course dispensed with the airless formality of that court; Dad lets real breezes in to trouble the gold leaves and keeps us all anguished with expectation. Whom will he take to his bed tonight? Who will be the butt of his jokes? Will he be expansive and, throwing a mantilla over his bald dome, jump up and join the gypsies in a fandango, shedding clothes until he's nothing but a fat man heaving under bits of black lace, the vertical scar across his chest pink and gleaming? Or will someone's remark, either ill-intentioned or misunderstood, spoil his fun? When his fun has been spoiled he becomes violent, throws Linda off the balcony into the sulfurous pool, breaks windows, charges at guests with carving knives, brays, and plays a record of "Night on Bald Mountain" at top volume. Then, spent and sulking, he huddles in a corner until those he has terrorized come one by one to beg his forgiveness.

"Just think," he says as we walk through the terraced gardens of the Alhambra, "here's the place where the Moors kept their Desd-de-demonas captive. We're shocked, of course," and at this point he puts an arm around my bony shoulders. "But that betrays our limited Christian point of view." Contained within his white suit and vest and bearing his black walking stick chased in silver, just now he does appear plausibly Christian. His beard was freshly trimmed and perfumed this morning, and his baldness is hidden by a panama hat, yellow band to match his tie; he looks respectable, years younger, a serious man willing to forgive Moorish excesses he could never commit. We are all drawn in by his reasonable, ruminating way of speaking and of planting periods at the ends of sentences by grinding the ferrule of his stick into the gravel. Christianity seems now a welcome limitation and I, too, regard the wicked Moors with tolerance. Even our little band of cardsharps, whores and layabouts grows complacent. We continue our struggle across the glaring gardens.

"If this were all mine," my father declares with quiet fervor, indicating the palace and grounds and including in his sweeping gesture even the distant facade of the Washington Irving Hotel, "I would make you—" he turns to me, tears in his eyes, which are dilated and peaceful after this morning's dose of Veronal—"you'd be lord and master of half my domain. You'd have slaves of your own, women—a whole harem of women!" Could he be hallucinating, I wonder.

His tongue flickers over his dry, rosy lips. He blinks and frowns. A chubby finger pulls at his shirt collar. "But maybe you don't want a harem of women." His eyes swim gently toward me. "We're all worldly, you can tell us. What is your preference? The fair sex, by which I mean men, since no woman ever treated *me* fairly. Do you prefer the fair sex, son?"

The people around me are mildly curious; I can't guess what my father wants to hear. Not for a moment do I wonder what a true reply to his question might be; I only want to preserve his equanimity and our semblance of . . . normality, I suppose. Yes. Normality. I long for us to be ordinary citizens sightseeing, soundhearing, scentsmelling, the decent bourgeoisie of only the usual five senses inspecting the grounds of a national shrine. "I'm not sure," I whisper, "but I think I prefer men."

My father is immensely relieved. He pinches my cheek and smiles. The time-wasters, touched by this domestic scene, work up their own smiles. Even Linda favors us with an upward tilt of her lips. "Yes, my boy," Daddy says, taking my arm, "I thought you were unnaturally fond of me. Don't worry about it. We're all open-minded. Don't worry one bit. I can take care of enough women for both of us." The retinue nods and beams at the obvious and serene wisdom of it all.

Now I can see that my father kept his miserable little company in tow by paying out the two most common leads—money and excitement. The Lindas and Pepes were poor and too lazy or pretentious to work. He provided everything—food, shelter, drugs and finery. And they were a bored, bickering lot; he amused them by planning events. Distractions of any sort would do, a cock-fight (gory spurs and flayed wings) as well as a swim off a rented power

104

boat or a fast drive through rain to the historic
caves or a quiet evening at home with just heroin, a
few records and the enema bag. His companions
were incapable of devising their own amusements
and relied on Dad to pick the fun and pay for it.
He alone had strong preferences. They had spent
so much time accommodating capricious patrons
that they had ended up with no caprices of their
own. Only Dad could really care to see Aranjuez by
moonlight and only he would organize the outing.
But as soon as we knew about the trip, then we all
went into action wondering what to wear and
squabbling over who would sit in the first car, who
in the second, whose turn it was to provide
sandwiches or mix the thermos of cocktails. So
eager were we to receive his favors that no one—I
least of all—stopped to consider whether they were
worth winning.

Linda was the reigning mistress, and we were all
required to defer to her. She presided over the table, at the formal beginning of supper if not at the
riotous end. In the evening when we descended on
the town, it was Linda who took Pop's arm during
the *paseo* and received the bows of the local men
and the women's snubs. And she had pride of place
beside Dad when we went motoring. If Dad needed
a pretext for evasion, he'd use her ("I can't accept
your kind invitation till I've consulted the lovely
Linda. She rules me in everything. A disgusting
sight—the uxorious man—but what can I do?").

Yet Linda reigned rather than ruled, a
figurehead with the figure if not the head for a posi-
tion imperiled every week by a new rival, usually

younger. "Juanita has come to stay with us for a few days," Dad would announce as he guided to the breakfasters lounging by the pool his latest discovery whose high-breasted body, tremblingly erect, and eyes, brown and shiny as burnt sugar, reminded me of no one so much as my dead mother. The court evaluated Juanita rapidly. They propped themselves up on elbows to examine her. One person rooted around in a purse for glasses and then submitted her to close inspection, another circled her to determine if she had what we called "back interest," a third scurried off to find out which room Dad had assigned the guest. After addressing her in Spanish, Pepe told Linda that Juanita was certifiably a slum child of Barcelona. Linda, tragic, superb, mounted the diving board, sliced into the water without a ripple and swam three lengths, suave as an otter.

By suppertime a change could be sensed blowing up off the bay, twisting the torch flames to light our faces and bodies from odd angles. Dad was subdued and polite beside Juanita, whispering to her as though he were just a guy on a date and the rest of us nosy strangers. Helene had listened at Juanita's door during the siesta and had informed everyone, with sympathy and malice, that Papa had "done her the honor." While we dragged a conversation in leaking buckets up the steep slope of the night, Dad and his new friend bubbled merrily like frisking kids under a rainspout. During our many pauses for breath we could hear them murmuring about—what was it now? The Spanish male. Does he make a good lover? Is he dependable marriage material? Of course Dad defended the poor, hypothetical devil, while reluctantly granting the creature is more gifted at conquest than occupation. His defense exasperated Juanita: "But the Spanish man is a child! Only you Anglo-Saxon men are real men. Only you take us seriously and make us your friends. The Spanish man wants a slave to cook his dinner and a madonna to raise his children." What could be more delicious than listening to a beautiful woman denounce her countrymen in favor of a man, a certain Anglo-Saxon man, much like oneself? Linda could not resist correcting her. "Slavery is better than neglect," she said. Juanita peeled an orange with a knife and fork and fed pungent wedges to my father. "Only vulgar people eat an orange like that," Pepe assured us. He, I suspected, knew he'd been boring Dad with his mimed re-enactments of old bullfights, his learned discussions of impotence, and the solemnity with which he approached cocaine; Pepe's only chance of staying on at "Top Boy" (the name of our villa) was by befriending Linda who, now that we'd finally left the table, played straight through "Für Elise," her one song, a recital piece from her girlhood in Corpus Christi—and then arranged herself beside me on pillows and pressed her head to mine, ear to ear. "See, Pepe, the little man and I are both so blond, we could be related. I *feel* related to you, honey," she said, ungluing herself and looking me in the eye with the humorlessness of a sheeted Baptist preparing for immersion, "and I think our souls are very, very close, you know?" She transfixed Dad with a glance; why did he court this lady before our envious eyes—and what eyes! Blue eyes red with weeping; black eyes so large they've crowded out the whites; eyes glistening like hot spills of sealing wax, still unimpressed; and my scanning eyes looking at Linda, Juanita, Linda, Juanita, father, father, my treacherous father.

And what was I feeling, you ask, as I nestled against Linda in that room while Dad did a two-step on the terrace with the Spanish beauty? Or when I stretched a match to Juanita's cigarette and Dad blew it out, then offered her the thick blue flame of his own smelly lighter? What did I feel when he and Linda fought bitterly the next afternoon by the pool? They paced around me. Linda sat on my chaise and ran an unconscious hand through my hair, as though my hair were her bright, accumulated grief. Dad chopped at the air with a hand bursting out of its fine pink glove of skin. A chair fell over, glass and blood were on the terra-cotta tiles, silences, shorter and shorter, contracted like birth pangs, a slap and a cry rang out—I begged them to stop it. Linda nursed her jaw and my father confided loudly to me, "You see, son, Linda doesn't understand the difference between commitment and attraction. I'm *committed* to Linda. I'm only *attracted* to Juanita."

For some reason Linda found the distinction consoling. She looked up through the mesh of her hat brim and asked, "Are you sure?"

"Sure I'm sure." My father rubbed his eyes and then frowned, as though, assured as he might be, he was nonetheless uncertain as to what subject they were discussing. His attention span seemed very short. Several times when he'd been winding up an angry peroration he'd lost the thread—and hurtled off into another tirade, its subject suggested by the last word he'd happened to say, its emotion dictated by the fortuitous subject. Today's drug, or combination of drugs, had sent the other inhabitants to their rooms on erring, sonambulistic feet. I'd observed Pepe cursing and mumbling as he careened from wall to wall in the corridor. Helene I found beached on the floor outside her room, awake and talking to herself but with no desire to press on toward bed. The chemical banderillas, which had felled the others, only confused my Pop, who dropped his head from its hump and trotted in circles.

On the third day of Juanita's visit her protector—no, her impresario—drew me aside and asked me to stop calling him "Dad."

"*Father*? Would that be better?"

"What?" He laughed and grew serious. "No, my boy, call me by name. We're friends as much as relatives. Besides, Juanita has such a morbid distaste for men over . . . forty. And you, my dear, are such a very *old*-looking sort of son for me to be having. Not that you look your age," he hastened to assure me. "Not a bit. You look no more than . . . *twelve*." The figure seemed to please him with its apostolic good sense. "Twelve," he repeated. "And how old are you, by the way?"

Though I was sixteen or seventeen I lied to comfort him and said, "Thirteen."

"No matter. But let's drop the 'Dad' and 'Pop' business, all right? 'Father' is no better, with its priggish sound—sounds like after church. 'Papa' is

obviously too immigrant, don't you think?" He was
smiling over his offhand way of dismissing all these
forms of address; he was sounding like his English
friend, Henry. "And 'Daddy' reeks of incest. No,
best use my name. Far more twentieth-century."
Our century always reminded him of science, which
in turn summoned up the image of his favorite
Swiss clinic where he had his blood circulated
through a chrome machine once a year and
"scrubbed."

When it suited him, Dad pretended he knew no
Spanish. Linda or Pepe was left with the job of in-
structing the maids, arranging trips, dealing with
visitors, answering invitations. But when he needed
to he could make his wishes felt, as they were on
the evening the time-wasters returned from the
paseo to find their bags packed and lined up in the
hall.

"What's this?" Pepe asked, his real eye rolling.
"Are we all off on a surprise outing?"

"Not all of us," Dad answered politely.

"Where's Linda?"

"She went off in a huff," Helene said.

"Hired, no doubt," my father whispered. Pepe's
live eye happened to align with the glass one and
both fixed me.

Now, whenever I hear the word *humiliation* I picture the chauffeur's faultlessly white gloves lifting
that pitiful, motley luggage into the trunk: Pepe's
small tan valise striped in faded red, one of its
clasps refusing to snap shut; Helene's shiny
nothings leaking out of a paper bag; Linda's green
metal trunk covered with stickers (a Moroccan

110

Touriste stamp beneath two fluent Arabic squiggles rising like thin hands in prayer out of gathered sleeves—memento of a hash run to Tangier; a battered decal of the Corpus Christi "Whips," her high school football team; a red, white and blue chevron from a French liner, reminder of that crossing during which she and her favorite warlock had propitiated the sea with an eighth of a teaspoon of his semen; stickers from Hot Springs, Arkansas and Baden-Baden—a mini-history of a mini-life).

Eventually Linda appeared and eventually her tears, reproaches and threats burst forth; the crickets all around us sounded like tiny bacchantes angrily shaking hundreds of tambourines as they marched toward the light and us, thirsty for a man's blood. The chauffeur, Jorge, "helped" a spitting, clawing Linda into the car; she rolled down the window and shouted back at Dad, "Okay, you bastard, you win this round."

Dad led Juanita and me back into the dimmed, polished house. "Hate a guest who *lingers*," he said.

I expected intimacy to steal over the house now that we were alone. The time-wasters had been thinned out, I assumed, to give Juanita room to sink her roots and spread her branches. On the stage, once the chorus has exited stomping and shouting, the lights concentrate to a blue spot on the lovers; I readied myself to listen to a tender duet, though I knew I'd hear it only in snatches as the couple stumbled drunkenly through the darkened house or fell silent over supper, their hands motionless while their concealed legs squirmed under the cloth. Or I knew I'd pick up a few faint notes when

111

the grownups retired for the *second* siesta of the afternoon and set their own crickets singing. I would become what their eyes, heavy with exhausted lust, rested upon across the swimming pool. I hoped I would be the innocent-appearing number superscribed above their numerals, raising them to a bewildering power.

But that didn't happen. Juanita wandered about the house alone in nervous high heels, sighing and trying her curly hair a different way in front of each mirror—a bun in the stolid rectangle framed in blackened mahogany; a seductive swoop over one eye before the silvery circle set in aquamarine tiles; spit curls in her oval vanity glass. My father grew paler and duller. When Henry, the English boy, joined us by the pool, Dad would wait only a few minutes before leading him into the house. Every day the pause before leaving us shortened. One day Dad grabbed Henry at the gate and steered him inside, angrily whispering something. Juanita snorted through her broad nose and subjected her tanning shoulders to another close look. She unhooked her bra and turned on her stomach. My job was to oil her skin, to stroke a sheen down that smooth, tense back, to feel the hot silk slide over shoulder blades and ribs as delicate as my own, to admire the nacreous hollow where her spine dove and drowned in the rising swells of her buttocks. She fell asleep cupping her breasts with her hands. As she relaxed the right hand opened and flopped to the ground.

Before long Henry was coming every morning and night, then morning, noon and night. At lunch one day Juanita was missing. My father, composed,

imperturbable, explained that her native Barcelona
had called her. He admitted that one's homeland so
often exerted a compelling spell over the vagabond,
no matter how far one might . . . and he dozed off
into his soup. Jorge and I dragged his body, which
seemed willfully heavy, back to his dirty, shuttered
bedroom. Bits of cotton littered the floor.

Henry moved in. He brought only his cheery
smile and a knapsack containing glassine envelopes.
In a bazaar somewhere he'd picked up a thin white
cotton shirt, which he wore constantly but never
washed. Since he kept himself tan if not tidy and
was very young, his dirt became something like a
"look," as though a soot streak on his face, twin to
the smudge on his hand, or the black crescents
under his nails, even his Benedictine smell, distilled
from grass, anise, clay and gin, came together into a
charming new fauve style.

Henry would shrink back rather than touch another
human being, he never swam or listened to records
and he missed meals. Nothing interested him beyond his own straightforward rendition of
"Greensleeves," which he whistled every evening at
five from within his canopied chair. When he spoke
it was in the outmoded dialect of Mayfair. When he
meant "yes" he said "rather" with an equal stress on
each syllable. He never looked at either men or
women with sexual curiosity. Once I passed him in
the hall as he came back from my father's bedroom.
He tossed his head toward the closed door, indicating Dad, and drawled, "Oh that kid." From time to
time he'd slip away for a day or two.

One night, while Henry was off on a jaunt, my

father came crawling into my room. He was naked and as disoriented as a wolf that has escaped a trap only by gnawing off its paw. He rolled over on his side next to my bed and groaned. Terrified, I knelt beside him, trying not to look at his body, scarred from waist to shoulder in a diplomatic sash of puckered pink silk. I held his beard-gritty chin in my hand.

"Tragic magic," he said, his name for heroin. "Too much. I shot up too much." He tried to move. "I can't hear anything. I played the gramophone at top volume—nothing. And everything is yellow. Henry's gone to buy me more d-d-damned junk." He winced. "More! May I sleep here?"

"Yes," I said, but he couldn't hear me. I bent down until I was in his range of vision and nodded.

He slept with his huge bald head on my chest and poked one fat finger into my mouth. Although I disliked the taste of his cold, salty finger, I submitted to it superstitiously, half-believing that my saliva was keeping him alive. At last he rolled away from me and began to breathe evenly.

All along, I suppose, I had wanted this passionate, ridiculous pasha in my bed, had wanted him to hold me in his legendary arms. But now that he was here, so reduced, I loathed him. The backs of my legs behind my knees became clammy. My hands froze. My mouth was unpleasantly dry, defiled by the taste of his finger.

I dressed and left the house. Running down the winding road past walled, unlit villas, I made for town. Once there I strolled the empty streets. A gypsy boy shined my shoes under a street lamp and then, without asking permission, briskly hammered taps into the rubber heels—an "improvement" he charged me for. I paid him without a word and tap-tap-tapped my way into the shadowy botanical gardens. I sat on a bench under a banana tree and cried. Someone put a friendly arm around me. It was you at last.

CHAPTER VII

When I came back to her, Didi was living in a palace that overlooked the ruins. Her paintings were in a new style, she'd married and divorced a husband since I'd last seen her, and her apartment was unexpectedly neat. Down below, tiny tourists labored across shimmering fields browned by the August sun but whitened in faint circles and squares by the jagged traces of temples emerging out of the ground in that way wisdom teeth erupt thorugh the gums. A group of Orientals glided to one spot and stared obediently at a foot ruler of half-buried marble, the dog's oldest bone; once we looked at it as you read from the guidebook: "This they regarded as the dead center of the world, and from this point they measured all distances. . . ."

Didi asked me about my life. I told her where I'd been, but her attention dispersed into minute droplets that condensed into a turbulent cloud just below the figured ceiling. "No, no," came the downpour, "say something real."

I invited her to set an example and she complied by telling me about the gypsy woman who had installed herself last winter in a wagon on the streets below. Didi had taken her food and blankets and then, on a cold night, brought her up to these rooms. Now Didi was pacing across the tiles in a studio where all the canvases were turned to the wall; when she paused the air was filled with the impassioned argument of traffic. In the distance I could see the ancient amphitheater, which looked like those clumsy plasticine molds, uppers and lowers, that dentists ask you to bite into. "She insisted on sleeping in my room. I moved to the day bed. Her old dog came with her and shit everywhere, on the chairs, under the bed. My maid quit. The gypsy said she'd been a princess and . . . I don't know. Could be. Her voice—" and Didi shifted into a bass register, musical and whispering, the words as precise and irresistible as the witch's invitation to the children—"was like this. Oh, what wonderful stories she told, all lies, but . . . I liked having her here, telling me her stories. I had to wait on her; she expected it. But she frightened me. And the dog howled and whined all night, dragging its paralyzed hind legs from room to room. The princess could be so jealous. She tore the phone out of the wall when I talked to somebody too long. I found her a nursing home but she didn't like it and she came back here. I put her in a boarding house, but the landlady begged me to take her back. Finally I forced her to go away, I had to call in a policeman—I, a communist! She ended up downstairs, back in her little wagon again."

The narrow wings of Didi's apartment folded around the dark heart, her bedroom. When she stood at the door of that soundproofed chamber, she warned me, "I will not emerge from this room for twelve hours. Nothing must disturb me. In the morning the maid will make you breakfast—don't talk to her, she's a chatterbox, though I like her. But remember, I must not be awakened. I sleep a full twelve hours." She kissed me on both cheeks, inhaling sharply on the second kiss; then she shook my hand and pulled away a second too soon, closing the bedroom door behind her without a glance back.

I had keys and could go out for a walk, which I did. For a while I talked to a soldier from the South. He was standing in the entrance of a tent lit from within by a kerosene lamp. All along the boulevard were other soldiers on foot or in jeeps; they were putting up bleachers for the parade tomorrow. At the end of the thoroughfare was a glowing ruin.

When I'd lived in this city, a year or two after you left me, there were so many winter nights I walked here from my apartment, with or without Anxiety. In December the streets and squares are empty after midnight. I step out into the cold and hear the last storekeeper blocks away pulling the metal gate down over his shop front. A cat with a torn ear slinks across the street. Once I turn the corner I can hear a fountain splashing irregularly as the wind grabs the water and lets it go. Fifty paces on and the narrow street widens into a square flanked by two churches, the one on the right scrubbed, the one on the left as splendid but its doors boarded up, verdigris mottling the facade.

As I worked my way up a road curving below the exposed caves of martyrs, I kept my glance from rising to the still more impressive monument hanging above me—I would waste time and ignore monuments, those treasures of time other people have saved. My grief was luxurious, and it took the form of idleness.

How did my day go? Wake up at noon, order two coffees from the bar, which were delivered by a twelve-year-old with legs strong from soccer and a beardless face flushed from his climb to Peter's and my eyrie. As I fished for money, the boy would push his long apron aside with a grubby hand, crouch and play with Anxiety. Then he would look around disapprovingly at the unmade bed, the dishes sticky with last night's snack, the liquor bottles and (as though reproaching our disorder with his exactitude) he'd count out the change to the last worthless tiny tin coin in a voice surprisingly loud and hoarse. Peter was soaking in a sunlit but dirty tub, his head thrown back and submerged to the ears, blond hair darkened and expanding in water that had a vivacity of its own—smashing points of fire and reflected blue sky. Peter's bony knees, losing their gloss as they dried, pointed to the ceiling. I put his foaming tan coffee in its tall glass on the wet tiles beside him.

That was breakfast, followed an hour later by lunch, a three-course ordeal for which we dressed and descended. If it was warm enough we sat outside under an umbrella and picked at our squid while Anxiety hugged the pavement in the oval shadow cast by our round table. People we knew ambled past, paused to talk, joined us—and another liter of white wine was ordered. Now afternoon was hard upon us. Since the stores, banks and markets were closed for three hours we had no option but to take in a movie, where I witnessed the mouths of stars from my country open only to speak in the language of this. Restless eyes, green and immense, squinted nervously, embarrassed by the booming, cultivated tones that were being emitted. The words continued after the lips closed—and I pitied the rhetoric tumbling out of those timid, sensitive faces. During the scene in which the hero walks through a dark field the auditorium sank into dimness; a businessman beside me lifted my hand and put it under the raincoat on his lap.

Oh, but now the supper hour was approaching. Peter and I had our naps to take, a fresh set of clothes to put on, phone calls to receive, Anxiety to feed. And, after the meal, which had too many courses, too many people, too much chatter, I'd find myself alone in a great square toward dawn. A guard in uniform wavers by on his bicycle, the headlight brightening with the fall of each pedal. Dirty marble breeds a dirty cat, a second cat. The moving cars speeding beside the river begin to speak in individual voices, grunting, declaiming, objecting, all engaged in litigation.

When friends from home arrived with their sober faces and pressed, unfashionable clothes, they politely ignored my starved body and velvet suit and asked me to take them sightseeing. We climbed stone steps in the noon heat. If I stumbled they'd grab my arm and invent an excuse for me. Once inside an old building too large for human beings we'd stare at plaster swags on a ceiling or watch pilgrims struggle up wood steps on their knees. At restaurants I knew how to order food—in that way I was serviceable. Also I was good at changing money. More steps, more monuments, black, varnished masterpieces inside chapels, teeth and bones—and finally my friends would leave. They were usually your friends, your "saints," and once I felt that you were sending them not to comfort but to torment me; the contrast between their health and my illness was tormenting, as was their knack at moving so quickly, even through the summer heat, from one pile of steaming marble to another.

This time I'm here only for a few days and I'm determined to remain energetic. The moment I order a second liter and turn my unfocused gaze upon the flickering crowd, the water that bathes stone giants, the pigeons—then I'll leave. Till then I'll tick off ten items every day on my list of sights to see.

Didi drives me one night down a walled, curving road that, no matter how we turn, keeps reappearing, same tree, same convent, same crossing, as though we were on a Möbius strip—until a sudden lurch and sputter projects us down a gravel lane into such darkness that only the treetops against the sky, velvet cut-outs pasted on phantomed silk, remind me that there are qualities of darkness paling all the way to the face emerging from the shadows to greet us and invite us in. Though I had imagined we were still within the city limits, this is obviously a farm: the smell of earth, moisture dropping from leaves, a cockcrow—and now the blazing door to the barn slides open.

People who know me come up to kiss me. A languor, as pleasurable as the oiled hairs of a fur collar ticking across an exposed nape, tempts me to relax into their affection. No matter that I cannot recall a single name nor be certain where I met this tiny girl with the uneven teeth, green spectacles and baggy work pants, her spirit leaping up out of her skin with every laugh, her arms luminous as vapor lifting off a wet log, nor that obese man with the shrunken hand and a peculiar way of choosing delicate, courteous turns of phrase so at odds with the fanatical application of his finger to his nostril—nor this young woman, our hostess, whose hair, though tousled, and clothes, though paint-stained, are too well cut to admit her into easy camaraderie with her bohemian guests. A woman I met in my country emerges from the kitchen, gray hair streaming back from a face red with drink, the pungent odor of her cigar enveloping her like the greatcoat of a cavalry officer from the last century as he steps into an inn.

The vividness of these impressions drains away. We've moved to an unlit garden and I'm offered a hammock slung between two trees. Once I'm in it the stretched bowl of fabric conceals the other members of our party from my view. The man with the deformed hand discusses the greatest novelist of the moment, a motherly creature who lives with ten cats in the center of the city and phones people everywhere and at all times of the night for bits of information for her epic. He had been playing Oedipus in a town in the North when she called him and asked him to find a farmer who would know exactly how you steal a pig—or, better, how a thief stole pigs during the last war. Would you use a sack? How do you silence the squeals? Tie the trotters?

My dear, since I left you I have heard so much talk, all studded with such a profusion of detail, gloves of mail slapping at my face. I picture my face as bemused, vacant, even sweet as those gloves do their work. When a life has ended and an unenthusiastic Lazarus is coaxed up out of the grave, he totters from here to there, strips of the winding-sheet still gauzing his eyes and ears, but through the cloth he can see the gloves, hear the talk and he reels before the swarm and insistence of the undead, their stories, the arrangements they keep on making.

The girl with the green glasses and leaping exhilaration whooped with laughter. I peered over the edge of the hammock and saw she was pointing up to the treetops. After a while I deduced she'd seen a bat or a flying mouse of some sort and its name in her language was the same word as *labia*—which became a general source of merriment. Food of some sort was served, though it was too dark for me to figure out what I was eating and I revised one theory after another: veal, eggplant, supreme.

But the gauntlets were moving again and new stories were told of this one who went there, said that, returned here, wanted more, accepted less until that one asked for these, traded those, lost all, recouped some. Sustained unhappiness, the sort I was entertaining, goes on too long to tolerate clarity. What it needs is the blur of fog on the side of the hill turned away from the morning sun, the composing fog that eliminates the tricky connections between objects so difficult for the painter to render (the emergence of a trunk from the ground, of a neck from the truck) and suspends in an enveloping medium only those elements grateful to the brush (the branch, the face). Drink dimmed the anxious clutter of detail, but after suppressing it ended up by shedding a lurid gleam on what remained. Best of all those agents of dilution is fiction—either the fiction of memory or fantasy—for it alone dissolves the entire scene in the cloud, brilliant or black, of desire.

The night swept in over me in soundless waves, but each breaker rustled away to reveal a jagged bit of bottle glass, an empty shell, a sand-choked carton. Now Didi and her friends, these people who appeared to know me and like me, were disputing the merits of sopranos—their diction, their phrasing, their vibrato, their range. I thought I saw the flight of a mouse from one branch to another.

Once I had moved out of your house I knew I wanted back in. Robert, the giant lover for whom I'd left you, became a fool overnight. His constant eating revolted me. He drank half a quart of milk a day and at one sitting shoveled in mounds of potatoes, meat, bread, vegetables—and sweets. My father had told me that desserts were only for children or the senile, and I clung to his unreasonable prejudice. Even Robert's vulnerability, too like my own, annoyed me. If he loved me it was because he knew no one else; I was his only friend and he was quite content to settle in with me.

For a month I wouldn't let myself phone you.

Whenever I was out walking I looked for you, but you and your friends had vanished. The bits and pieces of mail you forwarded came without comment. An attorney wrote me about the money you were giving me. That was all.

One afternoon I saw you dart out of a taxi into a shop and I followed you. A bell tinkled, the chocolates smelled so sweet, you straightened up from the counter and turned toward me—but it wasn't you, rather a quizzical stranger with a Slavic accent and a child's greedy penchant for sweets.

I knew I loved someone now, not exactly you but the freakish warm days of that winter, the reflections of traffic lights on wet pavements, the kindness of the unknown bartender who kept my glass full and wiped his hairy hands on his apron, the lyrics of songs on jukeboxes. As I wandered the city I found everyone touching and brave. Four twenty-year-olds out on a Saturday night, clustered in a corner of a bar and unsuccessfully suppressing the urge to dance, seemed heroic; they flirted with everyone who walked past them. Didn't they know (as I did) that the best thing had already happened, that their long lives, that progression from this year's hits and haircuts to next year's, from a first job to a second, a sixth, from sitting over cold coffee at dawn in a diner to sipping wine at supper on a balcony in Haiti—that this long sequence of slightly varying incidents would give them only time to see the past from every angle, as though the past were a statue they kept pacing around in ever-widening circles?

Your face swirled in a blur before my imagination, tones of color rose to greet a smudge of black, and then the focus sharpened and you were there smiling from under the funny carnival hat as you came out of the hotel and pretended surprise at seeing me. You ran toward the camera, jogging in place for a few seconds (or so it seemed) until you suddenly swarmed close, immense and dark; I froze the projector on a frame of your heavy-lidded eyes just as they went vague, a stray dazzle of sunlight in the lens casting a mysterious rainbow in the left pupil—then the film went up in flames.

After staying up all one night I stopped off at Robert's and showered, shaved and changed. In his ragged white terry cloth robe Robert looked like a large, molting bird. He opened the refrigerator and contemplated its racks of cold food for some time before asking me where I was coming from and where I was going. I told him I had to see you, that I had met someone on the pier who'd once given you a dog and that we had gone to his place and made desultory love but then plunged into an orgy of talk about you.

"Are you going back to him?" Robert asked, meaning you. He yawned with embarrassment and placed a slab of strudel in the oven to warm up.

"Who knows? I've got to see him. It just came over me," I said, mentally hearing one phrase over and over again: "Blame it on my youth."

The maid was glad to see me and said you'd run out on an errand but would be back soon. She seated me in the drawing room and gave me a cup of coffee. The phone kept ringing and I heard her taking your messages; obviously your social life continued to be a growth industry. Hampers of fruit and tinned things under yellow cellophane lined the butler's pantry; were you about to go on a trip? The furniture had been restored, the rugs laid, the white dining room was pale blue, paintings of a featureless but momentarily fashionable style that neither you nor I liked lined the hall and were making headway in the guest bedrooms. In your room two trunks sat, open and overflowing. The clothes in the new trunk were so small and chic; I picked up a silk shirt and held it to my chest. A perfect fit. The phone rang and rang. The doorbell rang and the maid signed for another delivery. Monogrammed towels hung in the bathroom, your initials twined around someone's. The blood leapt to my face and I slipped out silently as she raced to silence the phone again.

Didi and I left the party. Driving back down the lane, then over the winding roads into the city, passing hillside villas, swooping down on the domes of churches, sliding under triumphal arches, I felt my body becoming a reed, piping two notes, the mournful dyad. When I lived here the city was full of your absence. My longing played over everything I saw. But now even that loss has been lost, as the face of our Lord on a napkin might vanish one morning.

The next morning, before flying north, I went by the apartment I had shared with Peter. He's gone and the woman living there now has never heard of him; she was preceded by yet another tenant. As she talks my eyes stray toward the door leading out to the veranda; I half-expect to see Anxiety lying on the marble lintel, her forelegs and dozing head in shadow, her hindquarters in sunlight. But Peter, red-faced and vengeful the night I packed, swore to me that if I left him he'd put the dog out in the streets. She yapped and spun unsuspectingly when I stood at the door the last time with the Captain, who had come to rescue me and take me home. In a letter Didi mentioned Anxiety had been seen scavenging but had slinked away when Didi had tried to lure her into the car. One other time the dog, much thinner and limping, had been glimpsed from a moving bus.

That afternoon the boat enfiled the channels of the harbor, threading its way between upright clusters of pylons, asparagus in a steamer. We moved past an island and its deserted monastery. The aggressive smell of geraniums invaded the air. A grounded tanker marked the shallows. As we approached our destination more and more of the city blew across the sun-hammered tin top of the water, for the city's pastel and nougat colors had been lent to the outboards and sleepy barges drifting out to meet us, and its will to soar drove the gulls climbing the wind.

An ancient woman with blue eyes as fresh and wild as full pardon was shrieking to the helmsman in my language, "But surely you know where the Helvetius is. You must. I go across a large square—and then? And *then*? The Helvetius. Years ago I knew your language perfectly. Elveetyo? El-vaytoos? The Helvetius."

Obviously not understanding a word, the

helmsman and the crew shrugged and smiled at each other and stretched out their hands and juggled invisible fruit that was large and light, since it struck the palms gently and caused only the fingertips to curl. I came to her rescue; it was evident to me alone that this woman, despite (or because of) her torn dress, laceless sneakers and tangled hair, was either a duchess or a clairvoyant.

In translating for the woman and locating her hotel, I spoke to one of the boys—the one I'd seen dashing barefoot along the gunwales, the one I'd envied and despised for a health that made him smirk, self-satisfied, at the dirty foreign lady and then turn into the sun and shade his eyes with a raised hand that transcended self and dwarfed merely human satisfaction.

Following his directions I guided the duchess to the Helvetius. Her suitcase was no larger than a lunchbox and as light as her remaining sentence on earth. In the swarming alley outside the hotel she told me, blue eyes ecstatic and face lifted, that she had trusted God to send her an angel. She insisted on that word until my smile saddened, my lips released a scroll of gothic letters, and my shoulders broadened to support wings striped every color of the rainbow and lifted by long sheets of muscle anchored to an aching coccyx.

That evening, as the sun, frustrated with the day's painting, began to make a mess of it, I chanced upon the boy. He was in shorts, hosing down the boat. It turned out he lived with his family just across the canal from me.

Being with Sergius that long summer provided

me with another life—not an alternative to my real existence, which has no character, but to every evening's round of parties and melancholy adult pleasures. At night, ablaze in a white suit, I would saunter over the bridge to a palace where I would stand, secretly bathed in sweat, and talk to women about their antique jewelry, as I had done for so many summers, and on the way I might pass Sergius, who would be too intimidated by my suit, my companions and our conversation in a language he did not know to return my nod. But in the morning I'd step out through glass doors onto a narrow balcony and look up at his window. There he'd be, tan face jutting out over a pot of geraniums, harp strings of light, bouncing up from the water, rippling on his neck. We pantomimed our plan—his descent, mine, our meeting on the bridge.

His waking hours were spent in a prison of rituals and superstitions, his "mania," as he called it. I was forbidden to pronounce the numbers three and seven; they became "two plus one" and "six plus one." He could not pass a shadow on the pavement without turning his head to one side and spitting through his teeth, more a hiss than a spit. Crossing a bridge required several false starts, retracing his path, a full turn on the second step up, four hisses. The mere mention of death sent him into a fit of twirling sibilance. His grandmother, whom he escorted every evening to the levee for a lemon ice, was the only member of his large family not too ashamed to appear with him in public. His one friend was a short lad with dark circles under his eyes whose English teacher, in some zany moment, had assigned him, though he was a beginner, Whistler's *The Gentle Art of Making Enemies*; I had to translate a new passage every afternoon for this boy who accepted his nickname, "Gnome," without comment.

I was Sergius's protector. The demons would leave him alone for an hour if I was willing to take charge. "Am I your responsibility?" he'd ask me. I nodded. "Say it!" he insisted.

"You are my responsibility."

Then he'd smile.

To make me proud of him he told me about his conquests of German and Swedish and English girls, usually tourists who stayed in the small hotel next to his house. He demonstrated to me what a good swimmer he was by suddenly interrupting our walk, stripping to his underpants and plunging into the harbor beneath a gold weathervane held in the gold hand of Fortune atop the old customs house. He instructed me in the peculiarities of his dialect; its quaintness he appreciated so fully that I knew he had exposed these same trinkets to other buyers.

His one polite accomplishment was twanging a guitar and singing pop songs in my language; he had learned the lyrics by rote from a record. I was placed on a chair in a deserted storeroom the neighborhood kids had rented as their club headquarters. Sergius howled into expensive sound equipment, then asked me if I could understand the words. I couldn't. He'd mastered the intonations but scrambled the meaning.

We sat on grass, a unique patch of verdure in a city of stone and water, and he asked me how I could endure his mania. I told him allowances had to be made for me as well, since I liked men. He couldn't take it in. He assured me it was a scandal. He asked me if I'd tried girls and offered to secure for me the blonde in the floppy hat coming toward us. After a while he took my arm and said, as we began to stroll, "What a fine couple we are, you with your scandal, me with my mania."

I never touched him, though he took my hand once during a Kung Fu movie and whispered, "Am I your responsibility?"

"Yes."

"Say it!"

I felt again the happiness you gave me. The theater, a deconsecrated church, was squirming with amorous adolescents and raucous sub-teens, and in their midst I sat decorously, blushing with guilty pleasure, fearing that when the warrior annealed his steel fists in the fire the wizard provided, someone might have seen the boy's Midas hand in mine. A brat in pigtails kneeled in her seat and shouted over my shoulder at her accomplice whose black eyes had become pools of blue as the avenger flew in a magic cape and pounced on a bearded wrongdoer; I was caught in the crossfire of the kids' post-luncheon breath, but even those whiffs of garlic smelled like desire. "You are my responsibility," I said.

If I were to end with a movie, in it we would appear flying high against a backdrop of Spain. You had saved me from my father, you bought me a forged passport, you arranged our escape, you gave me a new name—yours. That name became my magic cape. In a second scene I'd show us standing by french doors looking out into a rainy garden irradiated by the blue-white sun. Schubert's *The Trout* is playing on the radio. I'm convinced I'll never be so happy again, nor was I until one midnight I gave you a dance class in a friend's studio. For once I had something to give, a skill I'd acquired during *my* brief mania for ballet after I dropped out of college. Your clumsiness I ignored (I knew how sensitive you were about your body), and when you laughed at your own mistakes I coolly announced the next combination. Admit that I handled that first class with a straightforwardness available only to the wisest lover or a perfect stranger. For an hour we centered, lifted, balanced with the curtains drawn over the mirrors. Only during the last ten minutes did I offer you the image of a man rediscovering his feet ("More turnout!") and hands ("Soften the fingers!") and shoulders ("Drop them!") and buttocks ("Tuck in!"). The excitement of one moment finds that of another, though they be years apart, and the theater full of children seething around an assumed responsibility detects its counterpart in the motionless leaves liquifying into light or the poised body of a man feeling his way back into his muscles. The instruments tune up and wait for him to begin.

Moralists say that our actions and not our intentions define us, and by that harsh rule I lose all definition. I longed away my childhood, resisted my youth, regretted the rest, and in that history appear, here and there, my protestations of good will and my pleas for redemption any serious historian knows to ignore. Nothing will come of my pleas and protestations, the outcome is in the stars, never more radiant than when they die, tyrannical novae.

CHAPTER VIII

Children in school uniforms sip lemonade and display a fearlessness I envy. This little boy, still flicking his head to one side between sentences though the long blond forelock that once excused the tic had been cut, boldly contradicts his father: "No, the *Empress* is the schooner, Dad." The father is unoffended by that high, clear voice and unimpressed with its mandarin accents, which are his own. And then the boy, who inherited his first name from a seventeenth-century theologian and his last from a nineteenth-century industrialist, runs off to play.

Japanese lanterns sway for the holiday over the drifting crowd; they are strung between clapboard houses in a square planted with elm and lawn. The ocean is only a block away, but the square has been laid out to exclude it, much as the manner of the summer people is calculated to ignore the water's moving plea for adventure.

My love, I write you from the island, where they're still talking about you. Dorothy sends her greetings; she speaks like you now, sniffing your ironic exhalation of a laugh through her nose, reeling off lines in conversation that could go right into a book or may have come from one, counting off points on her fingers, though she becomes confused in her organization and after A and B switches to 3. And, like you, she seasons the pedantry with a touch of irony that has worked its way through the whole dish. Still, she can be cruel, which you never were, and her irony disguises uncertainty whereas yours expressed sympathy—for my distractions, your quandary, everyone's compromises. And, unlike you, she can speak with authority to children. When they would ask you a question about anything factual (mosquitoes, say) you could answer easily and at length: "They breed on water, all two thousand varieties, and they can find it anywhere, in puddles, swamps, even in the internodes of bamboo. The females do not become fertile till they've tasted blood—it's only the females, of course, who drink blood." But should those boys or girls ask you what they should *do* (with their lives or loves), then you'd grow perplexed, find a spot on your trousers, smile, frown, search the sky for help, and finally— remember?—blurt out a sentence that began and ended with "But—." You were the apostle of the particular. If we'd be walking through the flower district at night you'd nudge me and nod toward a plate glass window: half-way back in the store, beyond a floor littered with ferns, were two bunches of tender purple gladioli in vases behind black metal bars, conspicuously padlocked. You'd whisper, "I'm sure they're innocent."

Everyone here is impersonating you. I, for one. I've mastered your way of asking the most personal questions so directly that they invariably surprise the truth out of the flattered, flustered person I'm

136

quizzing. Bob sits as you did, one leg draped over the other, hands in the air, head cocked to one side. Little Tom, no longer so little, has eyebrows like yours that slant downwards; if they were to join above the nose they'd form the Chinese character for *humanity, people* or *man*. If read in conjunction with the open mouth, they'd mean "the members of a family." These are family members, surely, for they ask after you, if only in the sense that "after" can suggest "loosely based on" an earlier model. Henrietta asks, "Do you watch much tee*vee* these days?" and, later, "Would you like a *hot dog*?" Both time she emphasizes these words, raising her pitch and volume until I gasp at her ventriloqual art; that was your way of dealing with the twentieth century. In Henrietta's mouth, this little vocal trick is as period as an old silk pilot's scarf stuffed into a new denim jacket. One young woman tells me she saw you half a dozen times at her uncle's parties when she was a child; everyone came to life when you entered the room, she says, though she thought you were nothing special. Your remarks were circulated, even a puzzling one, like a new but possibly edible fruit passed from one monkey's paw to another's. Because you drank too much, she says, you turned a whole generation alcoholic.

You'd be amused how many adults of both sexes claim to have been your lover. I'm lost in the crowd, my one distinction obscured by all these smoking torches. Belle—who stayed with us only that one summer, right?—remembers the visit as a year and has letters to prove it, or at least lend credence to her version of things. Let her have her year; it alone makes her interesting to young people. Oddly enough, her husband has staked a claim over another year, though we scarcely knew him. Strangest of all, the Captain, ordinarily so careful about his "standing in the community," won't deny rumors that he once shared your bed, and this grotesque possibility is discussed in front of his grandchildren, the infamy of the deed, I guess, redeemed by the glory of its perpetrator. Dody, of course, has written her book about you and lives off the spiritual if not the material royalties. The Baganda of Africa judged a man's health by the length of his shadow; you must be thriving.

If there were no teenagers here I'd feel easier. At least I'd still be the youngest one among your friends, who would still oblige me by clucking over my nutty ideas. Remember the summer I had us sitting on tatami mats and filled the house with plants you ended up having to water? An old porch swing hung on chains was all I'd permit in the drawing room; after it fell under the Captain's weight, pulling down half the plaster with it, I declared the devastation "interesting" and preserved it: two patches of exposed insulation above, one the shape of China, the other of France, joined by a sagging seam that represented the mysterious affinity between those two countries. I'm sure everyone pitied you for having to live with a mad boy. Now I'm sane and long since an adult. At dusk and from a distance I'm still mistaken for seventeen, though every step toward me adds a month, a year—until, at ten paces, three decades descend on me and I'm an adorable gnome. My looks don't bother me except in one or two respects. I relied on them for so long to draw people to me that now I have no way to start a conversation. And the innocence of my face used to forgive my nasty teasing; now I've had to put kindness into my voice and words.

Experience has taught me you were kind but powerless and that my struggle to make you punish me, save me, stop me, teach me was misguided. You do not hang over the storm, firm hands in a sunlit study grasping a glass ball black with turbulence. Minute electrical charges craze the swirling clouds, but the cool glass sphere silences the thunderclaps, which are translated to your fingertips only in the way tremors are felt in a spoon by someone stirring a demitasse in Switzerland when the earthquake erupts in Tibet. Last night you were the Dalai Lama again and we were standing in a train together, swaying on metal straps. A mother and daughter sit looking up at us. I want them to see that you love me (they've recognized you), and just before you get off at your stop you do touch my shoulder. We speed on above turning, screaming prayer wheels, sutras on paper slips fluttering from the spokes—

"Are you all right?" someone, perhaps, yes, Belle asks as she leads me from the dance floor. A crowd parts for us, their lips compressed, eyes averted; once again I'm the mad boy! I press the glass of lemonade to my forehead and go through the motions of pretending to recover from a dizzy spell. My clothes, I notice, are fine, the trousers clean, shirt dry, shoes on, and when I lower my hand from my face I'm relieved to see it's not smeared with grease or blood.

Back in my rented bed I read this passage from a letter by a Renaissance writer whose contemporaries called him "Divine": "As for myself, my eyes fill with tears when I remember how affectionately, in church and in the streets, the dear, sweet, lovely little Countess Madrina used to kiss me. The mischance through which I fell asleep beside her when I found her ill is now a stock scene of comedy . . . Alas, all these things are resolved into the air that carries away the sound of voices."

Picture the scene as you lie beside me in this single bed so lightly your side of the pillow isn't even dented. My father, though long since dead, is in the next room playing billiards with another man who holds the cue stick and watches twin serpents of cigarette smoke curl up the caduceus. As they stand back and contemplate the colored balls under the tent of scorching light, their faces are suspended in shadow, only the lining of their upper lips gleaming with an emerald-green plundered from the baize table. My father is one of those gloomy statues who guard the entrances of churches but when he bends down to make a shot, he changes from portal knight to gaudy dey, a ring on every finger and his bald dome shiny and veined.

I can hear families tiptoeing home through the night fog. An ice machine hums on the porch and from time to time the freezer ejects another shower of cubes. The yellow mosquito light outside above my door is snapped off; the darkness permits me to peek safely through the blinds at the patriotic bunting sopping up the fog. Another family, armed with a flashlight, glides past, the child in a yellow hood and raincoat. In the distance the Japanese lanterns still sway above the deserted square. A neighbor turns on a radio that blares news for no more than a minute.

Mother has always believed that travel is broadening, at least in the prospect, and for her now, deep in the folds of her tent hung with extinguished lamps and carpeted with a rug stitched in stylized elements from an oasis (a palm frond, a pomegranate, a fountain), the prospect has narrowed to the sliver of night seen through the parted flaps. She props her white cheek on a gemmed hand that smells of lanolin and rosewater and she sucks the mouthpiece of an unlit hookah; its water chamber bubbles and she tastes cold ash. In her imagination she turns over the miniatures of memory, then scatters them, so that each one overlaps and partially conceals the next.

I scatter mine, and see you climbing into my window after we fought, your spirit outstripping your clumsy body. Though I had resolved to be asleep, or, if awake, angry at you, I was awake and afraid for you. What else could I do but help you over the ledge? And here you are propped up in bed, reading, dawn leaking in through the curtains, your ashtray piled high with cigarettes, each a new anxiety you'd selected, tasted, discarded, all of them bitter, a few still smouldering. When you said, "This can't go on, can it?" all I could think about were the records. Who would get the records? Now I loved your records as much as mine. I could deduce from your face that you thought I was laughing at you. Or maybe you were disgusted that I considered my only loss would be musical—but the mind, my mind at least, threads its way like lace from knot to knot and the open eyelets *are* the pattern. The sun has bleached out most of the pictures at the beginning and the end of the album. Only those packed in the center are still vivid, and they are the ones in which the sultan sits in white robes with his beloved under a white arch against a night sky on which a scimitar moon has been painted in heavy gold leaf. Fruits, trees, and fountains in the garden beyond do not diminish in perspective. Rather, they remain large and distinct, crowding toward the viewer.

A billiard ball strikes another with a smart tap and the second rushes to its destination, sinks and rumbles through the subterranean workings of the table. In her tent a woman gathers pictures and returns them to a sturdy box lined with salmon-colored silk. In the fog two dogs call back and forth from one yard to another, Tim and Anxiety howling through the years, each filling the night with short, imperious yaps that test the depth, sound for echoes and, hearing none, hearing nothing but the antiphonal voice of the other animal, bark and bark and bark as though time were a burglar who could be frightened away.

I saw you many times after I left you, and you have to admit that we had some good evenings together. We'd talk about your new love or mine, and I think I was able to give you some excellent advice, though you never took it. I stayed over at your house a few nights and that meant a lot to me but not much to you, so I stopped doing it.

So many great men destroy the lives of those around them—lovers, wives. The wife imitates his extravagant vices at night but does not rise at dawn to pick her way through the party rubble to the study. She, too, consults the spirit world, winters in Greece, keeps odd hours, experiments with drugs, has a theory about evolution, hates Poulenc, listens to too much talk—but for her nothing comes of it. She becomes haggard and opinionated, while he stays pink-cheeked, curious, industrious. Eventually her enthusiasms narrow to macramé and vodka. Have I become your monster? Am I the ruined wife?

I was in Florida when Belle reached me at last. A man I'd just met had come home with me to the rented beach house. We had been engaged in violent sex (the violence was all in the things he whispered to me), and I debated whether to answer the insistent phone. I did. Belle asked me if I was sitting down. She asked me that twice.

"No, Belle," I laughed, "what does that matter?"

"Sit down," she repeated. I did. She told me that you had been ill for two weeks with bronchitis, which turned into pneumonia. Since you were very old you hadn't been able to fight it off. And you had died. And been buried. Then she told me at length and with real animosity all she had gone through in trying to locate me.

I thanked her and hung up. When I returned to the high, glassed-in room overlooking the beach the stranger asked me what had happened. He was very understanding and sweet—you would have liked him. He took me into the shower and bathed me and washed my hair, embracing me again and again. I cried so long I could hardly stand up under the assault of hot water. Then I poured us drinks and we talked for hours. Finally we made love after all; he was just as violent, even more violent than before, as though nothing had intervened; for some reason I was grateful.

After he left I put on shorts and walked along the beach and looked at the palms curving away from the ocean. My old adolescent feeling that it was odd to be a man rather than a woman, to live here rather than there, now rather than then, struck me again. I wanted to hurtle through space and time.

Satan stoops to make his opening shot in clouds of sulfur smoke; the cue ball, white as the sun, speeds across a green void and cracks open a firmament of colored, numbered spheres that roll to fill all the space we can ever know. The mother, sultana in a black felt tent, stoops to read the patterns woven into the carpet. She pictures lovers in that garden saying, each to each, "Happy are we within our sacred grove, two forms, perhaps, but one soul, one love. The dervish birds whirling within the trees wail songs conferring immortality. But bigger birds in paradise devour themselves with envy of that endless hour when we met and love, will laugh, have lost track of where we were, are—heaven? Iraq?"

I step out on the porch in bare feet. Gusts of fog hold me gently. I'm hungry but there's no place on the whole island still open at this hour, whatever the hour might be. It could be dawn already, but I can't tell—the weather will hide the light for hours. Everyone's asleep, tucked away in historic houses

144

under heirloom quilts, a whole community whose only aberration was you. Perhaps Belle or the Captain is dreaming of you or me, and I glide through this fog as I might through their brains. When you slept you rubbed your hand over your eyes and nose in one precise half-circle—like a cat washing itself.

I'm sure I must be a wraith in someone's head right now; so many people looked at me oddly this afternoon when I walked up from the ferry landing to the square, bag in hand. Of course I'd forgotten it was a holiday, though one glance at the bunting and lanterns, the bandstand and the glasses of lemonade, reminded me.

I danced with Belle, and as we twirled another fat face dawned above a dark shoulder, then one drew out of shadows into the lantern light, and yet another person, in heavy age drag, gave herself away by her laugh. Not the sound (she was too far away for me to hear her) but her manner of throwing her head back with abandon while her precise, businesslike hands fussed and tugged at her cardigan to keep it from sliding off her shoulders. They all came over to me, our ancient rivalries abandoned, the difference between my age and theirs no longer significant or (in the eyes of the children) even noticeable. We were just glad to see one another. Whenever we gathered together in twos or threes you put in a star appearance—at least it felt that way. Everything was done in remembrance of you. It was so strange playing out this little piece before indifferent young eyes, as though we were members of a secret fellowship, now dissolved, introducing bits of ritual into casual conversation, each word or gesture thrilling the initiated.

I can picture you standing in our midst, drinking, deferential, modestly listening to someone's shapeless story flung out before you—and then you say something cutting, shears snipping so many yards into a pattern.

The saddest thing, the thing that makes me groan and step off the hotel porch into the night, is remembering how *modern* we all thought we were way back then. Old money, old names, these old houses were the legacy we ignored. For us there was only the figure in the foreground, standing so casually and confidently, yours, peering out into the night with a dreaming calm, then snapping your focus back onto Belle or the Captain. What would you say next? All of history—the panes in the windows with their violet tints and trapped air bubbles—was just a nice place to visit, but the old law was being lifted by you, word by word, the prohibitions broken, and some festivals dropped from the calendar. From a high place, belfry or minaret, I can see the garden and the strolling sultan and the beloved, wearing green hoods, the color of paradise. They are small but perfect.

The fog dematerializes the harbor and the boats, each gemmed with one ruby and one emerald, then floats the image up again from the bottom of the developing pan, and I sit down on a stone step, my left knee creaking. The creak startles me into thinking how arbitrary it is to be locked into this century, this language, this skin, and I stare out at myself with the humiliated dignity of a Civil War soldier, his blue eyes eerily white, looking at the camera as though to say, "Here I am, nineteen years old, a bit hungry, trying to remember the name of an old school chum I haven't seen for years, my toes cramped in my left boot; I'm not afraid of the bee circling the photographer's hooded head, though it would be funny to see him jump up, stunned, toppling the tripod—oh, God, you out there, take pity on me, on my left sideburn fractionally longer than the right, on my strong hand upon the saber hilt, and on my last joke resolved into the air that carries away all sound of voices."

And just as Tim and Anxiety bark at each other through the fog, so I call out to that soldier: "But I have no pity to offer, since I, too, am dying, and someone saw fit to play the same prank on me, imprisoning me within an antiquated tot's body, lacing me into a straitjacket that holds my arms folded in resignation before the maddening vision of a man or god who has died, gone away or never existed save in the tense, opaque presences of those things and people who, by virtue of claiming attention but denying the understanding, of demanding love at the cost of rewarding sympathy, must be addressed as 'You.'" And indeed, after I have risen from the stone step that left its icy wet imprint on my skin and have resumed my prowl, the fronts of some houses congenially proclaim they are on my side, open to inspection, tolerant of what they see—they are all "I's" that speak to my experience, whereas other houses—incomprehensible, disturbing, yet brimming over with mysterious invitations to happiness or pain—they must be called "You." And the rest of the buildings on the island, that is most of them, are uncharged, and they are houses that want no pronouns.

Coming here on the ferry today I studied all the other people on the deck. The floor beneath my shoes pounded with the beat of the old engine and the air was pure with salt when it flowed but foul with gasoline and fish whenever we idled. The sea, an actress who'd had too much to drink, was everywhere at once, splashy, a swirl of ruffles.

The motor made so much noise no one could speak. We were silent and contemplative, seated or standing bodies, unmoving though the wind did its best to create the illusion of apparent motion by rippling our hair and clothes and placing us against a capricious, sluicing background. All to no avail, since the wind, like the confusion of angels around the throne of heaven, only emphasized the solidity of what does not move. As I looked at the other passengers, I could easily pick out those expressionless, intriguing beauties I address as *you,* those same faces, dark or fair, brooding or elated, whom I'd always believed I could love, even if I'd seen them only for a moment on a train or a bus or passing me on the street as I headed away from your dinner table, your saints, into the noisy, quickening night, its shouts muted by the containing glass sphere that you, or I, the magus, hold though it roll across a billiard table as green as the paradisal hoods of the sultan and his beloved within their garden, its pomegranate, palm and fountain besieged by mist and the howls of two lost dogs.